TALES OF
ALLAN QUATERMAIN
AND OTHERS

TALES OF
ALLAN QUATERMAIN
AND OTHERS

H. Rider Haggard

WILDSIDE PRESS

TALES OF ALLAN QUATERMAIN AND OTHERS

Published by:
Wildside Press
P.O. Box 301
Holicong, PA 18928-0301

Write for our catalog, or visit our web site for a list of
available books: www.wildsidepress.com.

CONTENTS

LONG ODDS

THE STORY which is narrated in the following pages came to me from the lips of my old friend Allan Quatermain, or Hunter Quatermain, as we used to call him in South Africa. He told it to me one evening when I was stopping with him at the place he bought in Yorkshire. Shortly after that, the death of his only son so unsettled him that he immediately left England, accompanied by two companions, his old fellow-voyagers, Sir Henry Curtis and Captain Good, and has now utterly vanished into the dark heart of Africa. He is persuaded that a white people, of which he has heard rumours all his life, exists somewhere on the highlands in the vast, still unexplored interior, and his great ambition is to find them before he dies. This is the wild quest upon which he and his companions have departed, and from which I shrewdly suspect they never will return. One letter only have I received from the old gentleman, dated from a mission station high up the Tana, a river on the east coast, about three hundred miles north of Zanzibar. In it he says they have gone through many hardships and adventures, but are alive and well, and have found traces which go far towards making him hope that the results of their wild quest may be a "magnificent and unexampled discovery." I greatly fear, however, that all he has discovered is death; for this letter came a long while ago, and nobody has heard a single word of the party since. They have totally vanished.

It was on the last evening of my stay at his house that he told the ensuing story to me and Captain Good, who was dining with him. He had eaten his dinner and drunk two or three glasses of old port, just to help Good and myself to the end of the second bottle. It was an unusual thing for him to do, for he was a most abstemious man, having conceived, as he used to say, a great horror of drink from observing its effects upon the class of men—hunters, transport riders, and others—amongst whom he had passed so many years of his life. Consequently the good wine took more effect on him that it would have done on most

7

men, sending a little flush into his wrinkled cheeks, and making him talk more freely than usual.

Dear old man! I can see him now, as he went limping up and down the vestibule, with his grey hair sticking up in scrubbing-brush fashion, his shrivelled yellow face, and his large dark eyes, that were as keen as any hawk's, and yet soft as a buck's. The whole room was hung with trophies of his numerous hunting ex-peditions, and he had some story about every one of them, if only he could be got to tell them. Generally he would not, for he was not very fond of narrating his own adventures, but to-night the port wine made him more communicative.

"Ah, you brute!" he said, stopping beneath an unusually large skull of a lion, which was fixed just over the mantelpiece, beneath a long row of guns, its jaws distended to their utmost width. "Ah, you brute! You have given me a lot of trouble for the last dozen years, and will, I suppose, to my dying day."

"Tell us the yarn, Quatermain," said Good. "You have often promised to tell me, and you never have."

"You had better not ask me to," he answered, "for it is a long-ish one."

"All right," I said, "the evening is young, and there is some more port."

Thus adjured, he filled his pipe from a jar of coarse-cut Boer tobacco that was always standing on the mantelpiece, and still walking up and down the room, began—

"It was, I think, in the March of '69 that I was up in Sikukuni's country. It was just after old Sequati's time, and Sikukuni had got into power—I forget how. Anyway, I was there. I had heard that the Bapedi people had brought down an enor-mous quantity of ivory from the interior, and so I started with a waggon-load of goods, and came straight away from Middelburg to try and trade some of it. It was a risky thing to go into the country so early, on account of the fever; but I knew that there were one or two others after that lot of ivory, so I determined to have a try for it, and take my chance of fever. I had become so tough from continual knocking about that I did not set it down at much.

"Well, I got on all right for a while. It is a wonderfully beautiful piece of bush veldt, with great ranges of mountains running through it, and round granite koppies starting up here and there, looking out like sentinels over the rolling waste of bush. But it is very hot—hot as a stew-pan—and when I was there that March, which, of course, is autumn in this part of Africa, the whole place reeked of fever. Every morning, as I trekked along down by the Oliphant River, I used to creep from the waggon at dawn and look out. But there was no river to be seen—only a long line of billows of what looked like the finest cotton wool tossed up lightly with a pitchfork. It was the fever mist. Out from among the scrub, too, came little spirals of vapour, as though there were hundreds of tiny fires alight in it—reek rising from thousands of tons of rotting vegetation. It was a beautiful place, but the beauty was the beauty of death; and all those lines and blots of vapour wrote one great word across the surface of the country, and that word was 'fever.'

"It was a dreadful year of illness that. I came, I remember, to one little kraal of Knobnoses, and went up to it to see if I could get some *maas*, or curdled butter-milk, and a few mealies. As I drew near I was struck with the silence of the place. No children began to chatter, and no dogs barked. Nor could I see any native sheep or cattle. The place, though it had evidently been recently inhabited, was as still as the bush round it, and some guinea fowl got up out of the prickly pear bushes right at the kraal gate. I remember that I hesitated a little before going in, there was such an air of desolation about the spot. Nature never looks desolate when man has not yet laid his hand upon her breast; she is only lonely. But when man has been, and has passed away, then she looks desolate.

"Well, I passed into the kraal, and went up to the principal hut. In front of the hut was something with an old sheep-skin *kaross* thrown over it. I stooped down and drew off the rug, and then shrank back amazed, for under it was the body of a young woman recently dead. For a moment I thought of turning back, but my curiosity overcame me; so going past the dead woman I went down on my hands and knees and crept into the hut. It was so dark that I could not see anything, though I could smell a great deal, so I lit a match. It was a 'tandstickor' match, and burnt slowly and dimly, and as the light gradually increased I made out what I took to be a family of people, men, women, and children, fast asleep. Presently it burnt up brightly, and I saw that they too, five of them altogether, were quite dead. One was a baby. I dropped the match in a hurry, and was making my way from the hut as quick as I could go, when I caught sight of two bright eyes staring out of a corner. Thinking it was a wild cat, or some such animal, I redoubled my haste, when suddenly a voice near the eyes began first to mutter, and then to send up a succession of awful yells.

"Hastily I lit another match, and perceived that the eyes belonged to an old woman, wrapped up in a greasy leather garment. Taking her by the arm, I dragged her out, for she could not, or would not, come by herself, and the stench was overpowering me. Such a sight as she was— a bag of bones, covered over with black, shrivelled parchment. The only white thing about her was her wool, and she seemed to be pretty well dead except for her eyes and her voice. She thought that I was a devil come to take her, and that is why she yelled so. Well, I got her down to the waggon, and gave her a 'tot' of Cape smoke, and then, as soon as it was ready, poured about a pint of beef-tea down her throat, made from the flesh of a blue vilderbeeste I had killed the day before, and after that she brightened up wonderfully. She could talk Zulu—indeed, it turned out that she had run away from Zululand in T'Chaka's time—and she told me that all the people whom I had seen had died of fever. When they had died the other inhabitants of the kraal had taken the cattle and gone away, leaving the poor old woman, who was helpless from age and infirmity, to perish of starvation or disease, as the case might be. She had been sitting there for three days among the bodies when I found her. I took her on to the next kraal, and gave the headman a blanket to look after her, promising him another if I found her well when I came back. I remember that he was much astonished at my parting with two blankets for the sake of such a worthless old creature. 'Why did I not leave her in the bush?' he asked. Those people carry the doctrine of the survival of the fittest to its extreme, you see.

"It was the night after I had got rid of the old woman that I made my first acquaintance with my friend yonder," and he nodded towards the skull that seemed to be grinning down at us in the shadow of the wide mantel-shelf. "I had trekked from dawn till eleven o'clock—a long trek—but I wanted to get on, and had turned the oxen out to graze, sending the voorlooper to look after them, my intention being to inspan again about six o'clock, and trek with the moon till ten. Then I got into the waggon, and had a good sleep till half-past two or so in the afternoon, when I rose and cooked some meat, and had my dinner, washing it down with a pannikin of black coffee—for it was difficult to get preserved milk in those days. Just as I had finished, and the driver, a man called Tom, was washing up the things, in comes the young scoundrel of a voorlooper driving one ox before him.

"'Where are the other oxen?' I asked.

"'Koos!' he said, 'Koos! The other oxen have gone away. I turned my back for a minute, and when I looked round again they were all gone except Kaptein, here, who was rubbing his back against a tree.'

"'You mean that you have been asleep, and let them stray, you villain. I will rub your back against a stick,' I answered, feeling very angry, for it was not a pleasant prospect to be stuck up in that fever trap for a week or so while we were hunting for the oxen. 'Off you go, and you too, Tom, and mind you don't come back till you have found them. They have trekked back along the Middelburg Road, and are a dozen miles off by now, I'll be bound. Now, no words; go both of you.'

"Tom, the driver, swore, and caught the lad a hearty kick, which he richly deserved, and then, having tied old Kaptein up to the disselboom with a reim, they took their assegais and sticks, and started. I would have gone too, only I knew that somebody must look after the waggon, and I did not like to leave either of the boys with it at night. I was in a very bad temper, indeed, although I was pretty well used to these sort of occurrences, and soothed myself by taking a rifle and going to kill something. For a couple of hours I poked about without seeing anything that I could get a shot at, but at last, just as I was again within seventy yards of the waggon, I put up an old Impala ram from behind a mimosa thorn. He ran straight for the waggon, and it was not till he was passing within a few feet of it that I could get a decent shot at him. Then I pulled, and caught him half-way down the spine; over he went, dead as a door-nail, and a pretty shot it was, though I ought not to say it. This little incident put me into rather a better humour, especially as the buck had rolled over right against the after-part of the waggon, so I had only to gut him, fix a reim round his legs, and haul him up. By the time I had done this the sun was down, and the full moon was up, and a beautiful moon it was. And then there came down that wonderful hush which sometimes falls over the African bush in the early hours of the night. No beast was moving, and no bird called. Not a breath of air stirred the quiet trees, and the shadows did not even quiver, they only grew. It was very oppressive and very lonely, for there was not a sign of the cattle or the boys. I was quite thankful for the society of old Kaptein, who was lying down contentedly against the disselboom, chewing the cud with a good conscience.

"Presently, however, Kaptein began to get restless. First he snorted, then he got up and snorted again. I could not make it out, so like a fool I got down off the waggon-box to have a look round, thinking it might be the lost oxen coming.

"Next instant I regretted it, for all of a sudden I heard a roar and saw something yellow flash past me and light on poor Kaptein. Then came a bellow of agony from the ox, and a crunch as the lion put his teeth through the poor brute's neck, and I began to realize what had happened. My rifle was in the waggon, and my first thought being to get hold of it, I turned and made a bolt for it. I got my foot on the wheel and flung my body forward on to the waggon, and there I stopped as if I were frozen, and no wonder, for as I was about to spring up I heard the lion behind me, and next second I felt the brute, ay, as plainly as I can feel this table. I felt him, I say, sniffing at my left leg that was hanging down.

"My word! I did feel queer; I don't think that I ever felt so queer before. I dared not move for the life of me, and the odd thing was that I seemed to lose power over my leg, which had an insane sort of inclination to kick out of its own mere motion—just as hysterical people want to laugh when they ought to be particularly solemn. Well, the lion sniffed and sniffed, beginning at my ankle and slowly nosing away up to my thigh. I thought that he was going to get hold then, but he did not. He only growled softly, and went back to the ox. Shifting my head a little I got a full view of him. He was about the biggest lion I ever saw, and I have seen a great many, and he had a most tremendous black mane. What his teeth were like you can see—look there, pretty big ones, ain't they? Altogether he was a magnificent animal, and as I lay there sprawling on the foretongue of the waggon, it occurred to me that he would look uncommonly well in a cage. He stood there by the carcass of poor Kaptein, and deliberately disembowelled him as neatly as a butcher could have done. All this while I dared not move, for he kept lifting his head and keeping an eye on me as he licked his bloody chops. When he had cleared Kaptein out he opened his mouth and roared, and I am not exaggerating when I say that the sound shook the waggon. Instantly there came back an answering roar.

"'Heavens!' I thought, 'there is his mate.'

"Hardly was the thought out of my head when I caught sight in the moonlight of the lioness bounding along through the long grass, and after her a couple of cubs about the size of mastiffs. She stopped within a few feet of my head, and stood, waved her tail, and fixed me with her glowing yellow eyes; but just as I thought that it was all over she turned and began to feed on Kaptein, and so did the cubs. There were four of them within eight feet of me, growling and quarrelling, rending and tearing, and crunching poor Kaptein's bones; and there I lay shaking with terror, and the cold perspiration pouring out of me, feeling like another Daniel come to judgment in a new sense of the phrase. Presently the cubs had eaten their fill, and began to get restless. One went round to the back of the waggon and pulled at the Impala buck that hung there, and the other came round my way and commenced the sniffing game at my leg. Indeed, he did more than that, for my trouser being hitched up a little, he began to lick the bare skin with his rough tongue. The more he licked the more he liked it, to judge from his increased vigour and the loud purring noise he made. Then I knew that the end had come, for in another second his file-like tongue would have rasped through the skin of my leg—which was luckily pretty tough—and have tasted the blood, and then there would be no chance for me. So I just lay there and thought of my sins, and prayed to the Almighty, and reflected that after all life was a very enjoyable thing.

"Then all of a sudden I heard a crashing of bushes and the shouting and whistling of men, and there were the two boys coming back with the cattle, which they had found trekking along all together. The lions lifted their heads and listened, then bounded off without a sound—and I fainted.

"The lions came back no more that night, and by the next morning my nerves had got pretty straight again; but I was full of wrath when I thought of all that I had gone through at the hands, or rather noses, of those four brutes, and of the fate of my after-ox Kaptein. He was a splendid ox, and I was very fond of him. So wroth was I that like a fool I determined to attack the whole family of them. It was worthy of a greenhorn out on his first hunting trip; but I did it nevertheless. Accordingly after breakfast, having rubbed some oil upon my leg, which was very sore from the cub's tongue, I took the driver, Tom, who did not half like the business, and having armed myself with an ordinary double No. 12 smoothbore, the first breechloader I ever had, I started. I took the smoothbore because it shot a bullet very well; and my experience has been that a round ball from a smooth-bore is quite as effective against a lion as an express bullet. The lion is soft, and not a difficult animal to finish if you hit him anywhere in the body. A buck takes far more killing.

"Well, I started, and the first thing I set to work to do was to try to discover whereabouts the brutes lay up for the day. About three hundred yards from the waggon was the crest of a rise covered with single mimosa trees, dotted about in a park-like fashion, and beyond this was a stretch of open plain running down to a dry pan, or waterhole, which covered about an acre of ground, and was densely clothed with reeds, now in the sere and yellow leaf. From the further edge of this pan the ground sloped up again to a great cleft, or nullah, which had been cut out by the action of the water, and was pretty thickly sprinkled with bush, amongst which grew some large trees, I forget of what sort.

"It at once struck me that the dry pan would be a likely place to find my friends in, as there is nothing a lion is fonder of than lying up in reeds, through which he can see things without being seen himself. Accordingly thither I went and prospected. Before I had got half-way round the pan I found the remains of a blue vilderbeeste that had evidently been killed within the last three or four days and partially devoured by lions; and from other indications about I was soon assured that if the family were not in the pan that day they spent a good deal of their spare time there. But if there, the question was how to get them out; for it was clearly impossible to think of going in after them unless one was quite determined to commit suicide. Now there was a strong wind blowing from the direction of the waggon, across the reedy pan towards the bush-clad kloof or donga, and this first gave me the idea of firing the reeds, which, as I think I told you, were pretty dry. Accordingly Tom took some matches and began starting little fires to the left, and I did the same to the right. But the reeds were still green at the bottom, and we should never have got them well alight had it not been for the wind, which grew stronger and stronger as the sun climbed higher, and forced the fire into them. At last, after half-an-hour's trouble, the flames got a hold, and began to spread out like a fan, whereupon I went round to the further side of the pan to wait for the lions, standing well out in the open, as we stood at the copse to-day where you shot the woodcock. It was a rather risky thing to do, but I used to be so sure of my shooting in those days that I did not so much as mind the risk. Scarcely had I got round when I heard the reeds parting before the onward rush of some animal. 'Now for it,' said I. On it came. I could see that it was yellow, and prepared for action, when instead of a lion out bounded a beautiful reit bok which had been lying in the shelter of the pan. It must, by the way, have been a reit bok of a peculiarly confiding nature to lay itself down with the lion, like the lamb of prophecy, but I suppose the reeds were thick, and that it kept a long way off.

"Well, I let the reit bok go, and it went like the wind, and kept my eyes fixed upon the reeds. The fire was burning like a furnace now; the flames crackling and roaring as they bit into the reeds, sending spouts of fire twenty feet and more into the air, and making the hot air dance above it in a way that was perfectly dazzling. But the reeds were still half green, and created an enormous quantity of smoke, which came rolling towards me like a curtain, lying very low on account of the wind. Presently, above the crackling of the fire, I heard a startled roar, then another and another. So the lions were at home.

"I was beginning to get excited now, for, as you fellows know, there is nothing in experience to warm up your nerves like a lion at close quarters, unless it is a wounded buffalo; and I became still more so when I made out through the smoke that the lions were all moving about on the extreme edge of the reeds. Occasionally they would pop their heads out like rabbits from a burrow, and then, catching sight of me standing about fifty yards away, draw them back again. I knew that it must be getting pretty warm behind them, and that they could not keep the game up for long; and I was not mistaken, for suddenly all four of them broke cover together, the old black-maned lion leading by a few yards. I never saw a more splendid sight in all my hunting experience than those four lions bounding across the veldt, overshadowed by the dense pall of smoke and backed by the fiery furnace of the burning reeds.

"I reckoned that they would pass, on their way to the bushy kloof, within about five and twenty yards of me, so, taking a long breath, I got my gun well on to the lion's shoulder—the black-maned one—so as to allow for an inch or two of motion, and catch him through the heart. I was on, dead on, and my finger was just beginning to tighten on the trigger, when suddenly I went blind—a bit of reed-ash had drifted into my right eye. I danced and rubbed, and succeeded in clearing it more or less just in time to see the tail of the last lion vanishing round the bushes up the kloof.

"If ever a man was mad I was that man. It was too bad; and such a shot in the open! However, I was not going to be beaten, so I just turned and marched for the kloof. Tom, the driver, begged and implored me not to go, but though as a personal rule I never pretend to be very brave (which I am not), I was determined that I would either kill those lions or they should kill me. So I told Tom that he need not come unless he liked, but I was going; and being a plucky fellow, a Swazi by birth, he shrugged his shoulders, muttered that I was mad or bewitched, and followed doggedly in my tracks.

"We soon reached the kloof, which was about three hundred yards in length and but sparsely wooded, and then the real fun began. There might be a lion behind every bush—there certainly were four lions somewhere; the delicate question was, where. I peeped and poked and looked in every possible direction, with my heart in my mouth, and was at last rewarded by catching a glimpse of something yellow moving behind a bush. At the same moment, from another bush opposite me out burst one of the cubs and galloped back towards the burnt pan. I whipped round and let drive a snap shot that tipped him head over heels, breaking his back within two inches of the root of the tail, and there he lay helpless but glaring. Tom afterwards killed him with his assegai. I opened the breech of the gun and hurriedly pulled out the old case, which, to judge from what ensued, must, I suppose, have burst and left a portion of its fabric sticking to the barrel. At any rate, when I tried to get in the new cartridge it would only enter half-way; and—would you believe it?—this was the moment that the lioness, attracted no doubt by the outcry of her cub, chose to put in an appearance. There she stood, twenty paces or so from me, lashing her tail and looking just as wicked as it is possible to conceive. Slowly I stepped backwards, trying to push in the new case, and as I did so she moved on in little runs, dropping down after each run. The danger was imminent, and the case would not go in. At the moment I oddly enough thought of the cartridge maker, whose name I will not mention, and earnestly hoped that if the lion got *me* some condign punishment would overtake *him.* It would not go in, so I tried to pull it out. It would not come out either, and my gun was useless if I could not shut it to use the other barrel. I might as well have had no gun.

"Meanwhile I was walking backward, keeping my eye on the lioness, who was creeping forward on her belly without a sound, but lashing her tail and keeping her eye on me; and in it I saw that she was coming in a few seconds more. I dashed my wrist and the palm of my hand against the brass rim of the cartridge till the blood poured from them—look, there are the scars of it to this day!"

Here Quatermain held up his right hand to the light and showed us four or five white cicatrices just where the wrist is set into the hand.

"But it was not of the slightest use," he went on; "the cartridge would not move. I only hope that no other man will ever be put in such an awful position. The lioness gathered herself together, and I gave myself up for lost, when suddenly Tom shouted out from somewhere in my rear—

"'You are walking on to the wounded cub; turn to the right.'

"I had the sense, dazed as I was, to take the hint, and slewing round at right-angles, but still keeping my eyes on the lion-ess, I continued my backward walk.

"To my intense relief, with a low growl she straightened herself, turned, and bounded further up the kloof.

"'Come on, Inkoos,' said Tom, 'let's get back to the waggon.'

"'All right, Tom,' I answered. 'I will when I have killed those three other lions,' for by this time I was bent on shooting them as I never remember being bent on anything before or since. 'You can go if you like, or you can get up a tree.'

"He considered the position a little, and then he very wisely got up a tree. I wish that I had done the same.

"Meanwhile I had found my knife, which had an extractor in it, and succeeded after some difficulty in pulling out the car-tridge which had so nearly been the cause of my death, and re-moving the obstruction in the barrel. It was very little thicker than a postage-stamp; certainly not thicker than a piece of writ-ing-paper. This done, I loaded the gun, bound a handkerchief round my wrist and hand to staunch the flowing of the blood, and started on again.

"I had noticed that the lioness went into a thick green bush, or rather a cluster of bushes, growing near the water, about fifty yards higher up, for there was a little stream running down the kloof, and I walked towards this bush. When I got there, however, I could see nothing, so I took up a big stone and threw it into the bushes. I believe that it hit the other cub, for out it came with a rush, giving me a broadside shot, of which I promptly availed myself, knocking it over dead. Out, too, came the lioness like a flash of light, but quick as she went I managed to put the other bullet into her ribs, so that she rolled right over three times like a shot rabbit. I instantly got two more car-tridges into the gun, and as I did so the lioness rose again and came crawling towards me on her fore-paws, roaring and groaning, and with such an expression of diabolical fury on her countenance as I have not often seen. I shot her again through the chest, and she fell over on to her side quite dead.

"That was the first and last time that I ever killed a brace of lions right and left, and, what is more, I never heard of anybody else doing it. Naturally I was considerably pleased with myself, and having again loaded up, I went on to look for the black-maned beauty who had killed Kaptein. Slowly, and with the greatest care, I proceeded up the kloof, searching every bush and tuft of grass as I went. It was wonderfully exciting work, for I never was sure from one moment to another but that he would be on me. I took comfort, however, from the reflection that a lion rarely attacks a man—rarely, I say; sometimes he does, as you will see—unless he is cornered or wounded. I must have been nearly an hour hunting after that lion. Once I thought I saw something move in a clump of tambouki grass, but I could not be sure, and when I trod out the grass I could not find him.

"At last I worked up to the head of the kloof, which made a *cul-de-sac*. It was formed of a wall of rock about fifty feet high. Down this rock trickled a little waterfall, and in front of it, some seventy feet from its face, was a great piled-up mass of boulders, in the crevices and on the top of which grew ferns, grasses, and stunted bushes. This mass was about twenty-five feet high. The sides of the kloof here were also very steep. Well, I came to the top of the nullah and looked all round. No signs of the lion. Evidently I had either overlooked him further down, or he had escaped right away. It was very vexatious; but still three lions were not a bad bag for one gun before dinner, and I was fain to be content. Accordingly I departed back again, making my way round the isolated pillar of boulders, beginning to feel, as I did so, that I was pretty well done up with excitement and fatigue, and should be more so before I had skinned those three lions. When I had got, as nearly as I could judge, about eighteen yards past the pillar or mass of boulders, I turned to have another look round. I have a pretty sharp eye, but I could see nothing at all.

"Then, on a sudden, I saw something sufficiently alarming. On the top of the mass of boulders, opposite to me, standing out clear against the rocks beyond, was the huge black-maned lion. He had been crouching there, and now arose as though by magic. There he stood lashing his tail, just like a living reproduction of the animal on the gateway of Northumberland House that I have seen in a picture. But he did not stand long. Before I could fire—before I could do more than get the gun to my shoulder—he sprang straight up and out from the rock, and driven by the impetus of that one mighty bound came hurtling through the air towards me.

"Heavens! How grand he looked, and how awful! High into the air he flew, describing a great arch. Just as he touched the highest point of his spring I fired. I did not dare to wait, for I saw that he would clear the whole space and land right upon me. Without a sight, almost without aim, I fired, as one would fire a snap shot at a snipe. The bullet told, for I distinctly heard its thud above the rushing sound caused by the passage of the lion through the air. Next second I was swept to the ground (luckily I fell into a low, creeper-clad bush, which broke the shock) and the lion was on the top of me, and the next those great white teeth of his had met in my thigh—I heard them grate against the bone. I yelled out in agony, for I did not feel in the least benumbed and happy, like Dr. Livingstone—who, by the way, I knew very well—and gave myself up for dead. But suddenly, as I did so, the lion's grip on my thigh loosened, and he stood over me, swaying to and fro, his huge mouth, from which the blood was gushing, wide open. Then he roared, and the sound shook the rocks.

"To and fro he swung, and suddenly the great head dropped on me, knocking all the breath from my body, and he was dead. My bullet had entered in the centre of his chest and passed out on the right side of the spine about half-way down the back.

"The pain of my wound kept me from fainting, and as soon as I got my breath I managed to drag myself from under him. Thank heavens, his great teeth had not crushed my thigh-bone; but I was losing a great deal of blood, and had it not been for the timely arrival of Tom, with whose aid I loosed the handkerchief from my wrist and tied it round my leg, twisting it tight with a stick, I think that I should have bled to death.

"Well, it was a just reward for my folly in trying to tackle a family of lions single-handed. The odds were too long. I have been lame ever since, and shall be to my dying day; in the month of March the wound always troubles me a great deal, and every three years it breaks out raw.

"I need scarcely add that I never traded the lot of ivory at Sikukuni's. Another man got it—a German—and made five hundred pounds out of it after paying expenses. I spent the month on the broad of my back, and was a cripple for six months after that. And now I've told you the yarn, so I will have a drop of Hollands and go to bed. Good-night to you all, good-night!"

HUNTER QUATERMAIN'S STORY

SIR HENRY CURTIS, as everybody acquainted with him knows, is one of the most hospitable men on earth. It was in the course of the enjoyment of his hospitality at his place in Yorkshire the other day that I heard the hunting story which I am now about to transcribe. Many of those who read it will no doubt have heard some of the strange rumours that are flying about to the effect that Sir Henry Curtis and his friend Captain Good, R.N., recently found a vast treasure of diamonds out in the heart of Africa, supposed to have been hidden by the Egyptians, or King Solomon, or some other antique people. I first saw the matter alluded to in a paragraph in one of the society papers the day before I started for Yorkshire to pay my visit to Curtis, and arrived, needless to say, burning with curiosity; for there is something very fascinating to the mind in the idea of hidden treasure. When I reached the Hall, I at once asked Curtis about it, and he did not deny the truth of the story; but on my pressing him to tell it he would not, nor would Captain Good, who was also staying in the house.

"You would not believe me if I did," Sir Henry said, with one of the hearty laughs which seem to come right out of his great lungs. "You must wait till Hunter Quatermain comes; he will arrive here from Africa to-night, and I am not going to say a word about the matter, or Good either, until he turns up. Quatermain was with us all through; he has known about the business for years and years, and if it had not been for him we should not have been here to-day. I am going to meet him presently."

I could not get a word more out of him, nor could anybody else, though we were all dying of curiosity, especially some of the ladies. I shall never forget how they looked in the drawing-room before dinner when Captain Good produced a great rough diamond, weighing fifty carats or more, and told them that he had many larger than that. If ever I saw curiosity and envy printed on fair faces, I saw them then.

It was just at this moment that the door was opened, and Mr. Allan Quatermain announced, whereupon Good put the diamond into his pocket, and sprang at a little man who limped shyly into the room, convoyed by Sir Henry Curtis himself.

"Here he is, Good, safe and sound," said Sir Henry, gleefully. "Ladies and gentlemen, let me introduce you to one of the oldest hunters and the very best shot in Africa, who has killed more elephants and lions than any other man alive."

Everybody turned and stared politely at the curious-looking little lame man, and though his size was insignificant, he was quite worth staring at. He had short grizzled hair, which stood about an inch above his head like the bristles of a brush, gentle brown eyes, that seemed to notice everything, and a withered face, tanned to the colour of mahogany from exposure to the weather. He spoke, too, when he returned Good's enthusiastic greeting, with a curious little accent, which made his speech noticeable.

It so happened that I sat next to Mr. Allan Quatermain at dinner, and, of course, did my best to draw him; but he was not to be drawn. He admitted that he had recently been a long journey into the interior of Africa with Sir Henry Curtis and Captain Good, and that they had found treasure, and then politely turned the subject and began to ask me questions about England, where he had never been before—that is, since he came to years of discretion. Of course, I did not find this very interesting, and so cast about for some means to bring the conversation round again.

Now, we were dining in an oak-panelled vestibule, and on the wall opposite to me were fixed two gigantic elephant tusks, and under them a pair of buffalo horns, very rough and knotted, showing that they came off an old bull, and having the tip of one horn split and chipped. I noticed that Hunter Quatermain's eyes kept glancing at these trophies, and took an occasion to ask him if he knew anything about them.

"I ought to," he answered, with a little laugh; "the elephant to which those tusks belonged tore one of our party right in two about eighteen months ago, and as for the buffalo horns, they were nearly my death, and were the end of a servant of mine to whom I was much attached. I gave them to Sir Henry when he left Natal some months ago;" and Mr. Quatermain sighed and turned to answer a question from the lady whom he had taken down to dinner, and who, needless to say, was also employed in trying to pump him about the diamonds.

Indeed, all round the table there was a simmer of scarcely suppressed excitement, which, when the servants had left the room, could no longer be restrained.

"Now, Mr. Quatermain," said the lady next him, "we have been kept in an agony of suspense by Sir Henry and Captain Good, who have persistently refused to tell us a word of this story about the hidden treasure till you came, and we simply can bear it no longer; so, please, begin at once."

"Yes," said everybody, "go on, please."

Hunter Quatermain glanced round the table apprehensively; he did not seem to appreciate finding himself the object of so much curiosity.

"Ladies and gentlemen," he said at last, with a shake of his grizzled head, "I am very sorry to disappoint you, but I cannot do it. It is this way. At the request of Sir Henry and Captain Good I have written down a true and plain account of King Solomon's Mines and how we found them, so you will soon be able to learn all about that wonderful adventure for yourselves; but until then I will say nothing about it, not from any wish to disappoint your curiosity, or to make myself important, but simply because the whole story partakes so much of the marvellous, that I am afraid to tell it in a piecemeal, hasty fashion, for fear I should be set down as one of those common fellows of whom there are so many in my profession, who are not ashamed to narrate things they have not seen, and even to tell wonderful stories about wild animals they have never killed. And I think that my companions in adventure, Sir Henry Curtis and Captain Good, will bear me out in what I say."

"Yes, Quatermain, I think you are quite right," said Sir Henry. "Precisely the same considerations have forced Good and myself to hold our tongues. We did not wish to be bracketed with—well, with other famous travellers."

There was a murmur of disappointment at these announcements.

"I believe you are all hoaxing us," said the young lady next Mr. Quatermain, rather sharply.

"Believe me," answered the old hunter, with a quaint courtesy and a little bow of his grizzled head; "though I have lived all my life in the wilderness, and amongst savages, I have neither the heart, nor the want of manners, to wish to deceive one so lovely."

Whereat the young lady, who was pretty, looked appeased.

"This is very dreadful," I broke in. "We ask for bread and you give us a stone, Mr. Quatermain. The least that you can do is to tell us the story of the tusks opposite and the buffalo horns underneath. We won't let you off with less."

"I am but a poor story-teller," put in the old hunter, "but if you will forgive my want of skill, I shall be happy to tell you, not the story of the tusks, for that is part of the history of our journey to King Solomon's Mines, but that of the buffalo horns beneath them, which is now ten years old."

"Bravo, Quatermain!" said Sir Henry. "We shall all be delighted. Fire away! Fill up your glass first."

The little man did as he was bid, took a sip of claret, and began: "About ten years ago I was hunting up in the far interior of Africa, at a place called Gatgarra, not a great way from the Chobe River. I had with me four native servants, namely, a driver and voorlooper, or leader, who were natives of Matabeleland, a Hottentot named Hans, who had once been the slave of a Transvaal Boer, and a Zulu hunter, who for five years had accompanied me upon my trips, and whose name was Mashune. Now near Gatgarra I found a fine piece of healthy, park-like country, where the grass was very good, considering the time of year; and here I made a little camp or head-quarter settlement, from whence I went expeditions on all sides in search of game, especially elephant. My luck, however, was bad; I got but little ivory. I was therefore very glad when some natives brought me news that a large herd of elephants were feeding in a valley about thirty miles away. At first I thought of trekking down to the valley, waggon and all, but gave up the idea on hearing that it was infested with the deadly 'tsetse' fly, which is certain death to all animals, except men, donkeys, and wild game. So I reluctantly determined to leave the waggon in the charge of the Matabele leader and driver, and to start on a trip into the thorn country, accompanied only by the Hottentot Hans, and Mashune.

"Accordingly on the following morning we started, and on the evening of the next day reached the spot where the elephants were reported to be. But here again we were met by ill luck. That the elephants had been there was evident enough, for their spoor was plentiful, and so were other traces of their presence in the shape of mimosa trees torn out of the ground, and placed topsy-turvy on their flat crowns, in order to enable the great beasts to feed on their sweet roots; but the elephants themselves were conspicuous by their absence. They had elected to move on. This being so, there was only one thing to do, and that was to move after them, which we did, and a pretty hunt they led us. For a fortnight or more we dodged about after those elephants, coming up with them on two occasions, and a splendid herd they were— only, however, to lose them again. At length we came up with them a third time, and I managed to shoot one bull, and then they started off again, where it was useless to try and follow them. After this I gave it up in disgust, and we made the best of our way back to the camp, not in the sweetest of tempers, carrying the tusks of the elephant I had shot.

*   *   *

"It was on the afternoon of the fifth day of our tramp that we reached the little koppie overlooking the spot where the waggon stood, and I confess that I climbed it with a pleasurable sense of home-coming, for his waggon is the hunter's home, as much as his house is that of the civilized person. I reached the top of the koppie, and looked in the direction where the friendly white tent of the waggon should be, but there was no waggon, only a black burnt plain stretching away as far as the eye could reach. I rubbed my eyes, looked again, and made out on the spot of the camp, not my waggon, but some charred beams of wood. Half wild with grief and anxiety, followed by Hans and Mashune, I ran at full speed down the slope of the koppie, and across the space of plain below to the spring of water, where my camp had been. I was soon there, only to find that my worst suspicions were confirmed.

"The waggon and all its contents, including my spare guns and ammunition, had been destroyed by a grass fire.

"Now before I started, I had left orders with the driver to burn off the grass round the camp, in order to guard against accidents of this nature, and here was the reward of my folly: a very proper illustration of the necessity, especially where natives are concerned, of doing a thing one's self if one wants it done at all. Evidently the lazy rascals had not burnt round the waggon; most probably, indeed, they had themselves carelessly fired the tall and resinous tambouki grass near by; the wind had driven the flames on to the waggon tent, and there was quickly an end of the matter. As for the driver and leader, I know not what became of them: probably fearing my anger, they bolted, taking the oxen with them. I have never seen them from that hour to this.

"I sat down on the black veldt by the spring, and gazed at the charred axles and disselboom of my waggon, and I can assure you, ladies and gentlemen, I felt inclined to weep. As for Mashune and Hans they cursed away vigorously, one in Zulu and the other in Dutch. Ours was a pretty position. We were nearly 300 miles away from Bamangwato, the capital of Khama's country, which was the nearest spot where we could get any help, and our ammunition, spare guns, clothing, food, and everything else, were all totally destroyed. I had just what I stood in, which was a flannel shirt, a pair of 'veldt-schoons,' or shoes of raw hide, my eight-bore rifle, and a few cartridges. Hans and Mashune had also each a Martini rifle and some cartridges, not many. And it was with this equipment that we had to undertake a journey of 300 miles through a desolate and almost uninhabited region. I can assure you that I have rarely been in a worse position, and I have been in some queer ones. However, these things are the natural incidents of a hunter's life, and the only thing to do was to make the best of them.

"Accordingly, after passing a comfortless night by the remains of my waggon, we started next morning on our long journey towards civilization. Now if I were to set to work to tell you all the troubles and incidents of that dreadful journey I should keep you listening here till midnight; so I will, with your permission, pass on to the particular adventure of which the pair of buffalo horns opposite are the melancholy memento.

"We had been travelling for about a month, living and getting along as best we could, when one evening we camped some forty miles from Bamangwato. By this time we were indeed in a melancholy plight, footsore, half starved, and utterly worn out; and, in addition, I was suffering from a sharp attack of fever, which half blinded me and made me weak as a babe. Our ammunition, too, was exhausted; I had only one cartridge left for my eight-bore rifle, and Hans and Mashune, who were armed with Martini Henrys, had three between them. It was about an hour from sundown when we halted and lit a fire—for luckily we had still a few matches. It was a charming spot to camp, I remember. Just off the game track we were following was a little hollow, fringed about with flat-crowned mimosa trees, and at the bottom of the hollow, a spring of clear water welled up out of the earth, and formed a pool, round the edges of which grew an abundance of watercresses of an exactly similar kind to those which were handed round the table just now. Now we had no food of any kind left, having that morning devoured the last remains of a little oribé antelope, which I had shot two days previously. Accordingly Hans, who was a better shot than Mashune, took two of the three remaining Martini cartridges, and started out to see if he could not kill a buck for supper. I was too weak to go myself.

"Meanwhile Mashune employed himself in dragging together some dead boughs from the mimosa trees to make a sort of 'skerm,' or shelter for us to sleep in, about forty yards from the edge of the pool of water. We had been greatly troubled with lions in the course of our long tramp, and only on the previous night have very nearly been attacked by them, which made me nervous, especially in my weak state. Just as we had finished the skerm, or rather something which did duty for one, Mashune and I heard a shot apparently fired about a mile away.

"'Hark to it!' sung out Mashune in Zulu, more, I fancy, by way of keeping his spirits up than for any other reason—for he was a sort of black Mark Tapley, and very cheerful under difficulties. 'Hark to the wonderful sound with which the "Maboona" (the Boers) shook our fathers to the ground at the Battle of the Blood River. We are hungry now, my father; our stomachs are small and withered up like a dried ox's paunch, but they will soon be full of good meat. Hans is a Hottentot, and an "umfagozan," that is, a low fellow, but he shoots straight—ah! He certainly shoots straight. Be of a good heart, my father, there will soon be meat upon the fire, and we shall rise up men.'

"And so he went on talking nonsense till I told him to stop, because he made my head ache with his empty words.

"Shortly after we heard the shot the sun sank in his red splendour, and there fell upon earth and sky the great hush of the African wilderness. The lions were not up as yet, they would probably wait for the moon, and the birds and beasts were all at rest. I cannot describe the intensity of the quiet of the night: to me in my weak state, and fretting as I was over the non-return of the Hottentot Hans, it seemed almost ominous—as though Nature were brooding over some tragedy which was being enacted in her sight.

"It was quiet—quiet as death, and lonely as the grave.

"'Mashune,' I said at last, 'where is Hans? my heart is heavy for him.'

"'Nay, my father, I know not; mayhap he is weary, and sleeps, or mayhap he has lost his way.'

"'Mashune, art thou a boy to talk folly to me?' I answered. 'Tell me, in all the years thou hast hunted by my side, didst thou ever know a Hottentot to lose his path or to sleep upon the way to camp?'

"'Nay, Macumazahn' (that, ladies, is my native name, and means the man who 'gets up by night,' or who 'is always awake'), 'I know not where he is.'

"But though we talked thus, we neither of us liked to hint at what was in both our minds, namely, that misfortunate had overtaken the poor Hottentot.

"'Mashune,' I said at last, 'go down to the water and bring me of those green herbs that grow there. I am hungered, and must eat something.'

"'Nay, my father; surely the ghosts are there; they come out of the water at night, and sit upon the banks to dry themselves. An Isanusi[1] told it me.'

"Mashune was, I think, one of the bravest men I ever knew in the daytime, but he had a more than civilized dread of the supernatural.

"'Must I go myself, thou fool?' I said, sternly.

"'Nay, Macumazahn, if thy heart yearns for strange things like a sick woman, I go, even if the ghosts devour me.'

"And accordingly he went, and soon returned with a large bundle of watercresses, of which I ate greedily.

"'Art thou not hungry?' I asked the great Zulu presently, as he sat eyeing me eating.

"'Never was I hungrier, my father.'

"'Then eat,' and I pointed to the watercresses.

"'Nay, Macumazahn, I cannot eat those herbs.'

"'If thou dost not eat thou wilt starve: eat, Mashune.'

"He stared at the watercresses doubtfully for a while, and at last seized a handful and crammed them into his mouth, crying out as he did so, 'Oh, why was I born that I should live to

---

1 *Isanusi*, witch-finder.

feed on green weeds like an ox? Surely if my mother could have known it she would have killed me when I was born!' and so he went on lamenting between each fistful of watercresses till all were finished, when he declared that he was full indeed of stuff, but it lay very cold on his stomach, 'like snow upon a mountain.' At any other time I should have laughed, for it must be admitted he had a ludicrous way of putting things. Zulus do not like green food.

"Just after Mashune had finished his watercress, we heard the loud 'woof! woof!' of a lion, who was evidently promenading much nearer to our little skerm than was pleasant. Indeed, on looking into the darkness and listening intently, I could hear his snoring breath, and catch the light of his great yellow eyes. We shouted loudly, and Mashune threw some sticks on the fire to frighten him, which apparently had the desired effect, for we saw no more of him for a while.

"Just after we had had this fright from the lion, the moon rose in her fullest splendour, throwing a robe of silver light over all the earth. I have rarely seen a more beautiful moonrise. I remember that sitting in the skerm I could with ease read faint pencil notes in my pocket-book. As soon as the moon was up game began to trek down to the water just below us. I could, from where I sat, see all sorts of them passing along a little ridge that ran to our right, on their way to the drinking place. Indeed, one buck—a large eland—came within twenty yards of the skerm, and stood at gaze, staring at it suspiciously, his beautiful head and twisted horns standing out clearly against the sky. I had, I recollect, every mind to have a pull at him on the chance of providing ourselves with a good supply of beef; but remembering that we had but two cartridges left, and the extreme uncertainty of a shot by moonlight, I at length decided to refrain. The eland presently moved on to the water, and a minute or two afterwards there arose a great sound of splashing, followed by the quick fall of galloping hoofs.

"'What's that, Mashune?' I asked.

"'That dam lion; buck smell him,' replied the Zulu in English, of which he had a very superficial knowledge.

"Scarcely were the words out of his mouth before we heard a sort of whine over the other side of the pool, which was instantly answered by a loud coughing roar close to us.

"'By Jove!' I said, 'there are two of them. They have lost the buck; we must look out they don't catch us.' And again we made up the fire, and shouted, with the result that the lions moved off.

"'Mashune,' I said, 'do you watch till the moon gets over that tree, when it will be the middle of the night. Then wake me. Watch well, now, or the lions will be picking those worthless bones of yours before you are three hours older. I must rest a little, or I shall die.'

"'Koos!' (chief), answered the Zulu. 'Sleep, my father, sleep in peace; my eyes shall be open as the stars; and like the stars watch over you.'

"Although I was so weak, I could not at once follow his advice. To begin with, my head ached with fever, and I was torn with anxiety as to the fate of the Hottentot Hans; and, indeed, as to our own fate, left with sore feet, empty stomachs, and two cartridges, to find our way to Bamangwato, forty miles off. Then the mere sensation of knowing that there are one or more hungry lions prowling round you somewhere in the dark is disquieting, however well one may be used to it, and, by keeping the attention on the stretch, tends to prevent one from sleeping. In addition to all these troubles, too, I was, I remember, seized with a dreadful longing for a pipe of tobacco, whereas, under the circumstances, I might as well have longed for the moon.

"At last, however, I fell into an uneasy sleep as full of bad dreams as a prickly pear is of points, one of which, I recollect, was that I was setting my naked foot upon a cobra which rose upon its tail and hissed my name, 'Macumazahn,' into my ear. Indeed, the cobra hissed with such persistency that at last I roused myself.

"'*Macumazahn, nanzia, nanzia!*' (there, there!) whispered Mashune's voice into my drowsy ears. Raising myself, I opened my eyes, and I saw Mashune kneeling by my side and pointing towards the water. Following the line of his outstretched hand, my eyes fell upon a sight that made me jump, old hunter as I was even in those days. About twenty paces from the little skerm was a large ant-heap, and on the summit of the ant-heap, her four feet rather close together, so as to find standing space, stood the massive form of a big lioness. Her head was towards the skerm, and in the bright moonlight I saw her lower it and lick her paws.

"Mashune thrust the Martini rifle into my hands, whispering that it was loaded. I lifted it and covered the lioness, but found that even in that light I could not make out the foresight of the Martini. As it would be madness to fire without doing so, for the result would probably be that I should wound the lioness, if, indeed, I did not miss her altogether, I lowered the rifle; and, hastily tearing a fragment of paper from one of the leaves of my pocket-book, which I had been consulting just before I went to sleep, I proceeded to fix it on to the front sight. But all this took a little time, and before the paper was satisfactorily arranged, Mashune again gripped me by the arm, and pointed to a dark heap under the shade of a small mimosa tree which grew not more than ten paces from the skerm.

"'Well, what is it?' I whispered; 'I can see nothing.'

"'It is another lion,' he answered.

"'Nonsense! Thy heart is dead with fear, thou seest double;' and I bent forward over the edge of the surrounding fence, and stared at the heap.

"Even as I said the words, the dark mass rose and stalked out into the moonlight. It was a magnificent, black-maned lion, one of the largest I had ever seen. When he had gone two or three steps he caught sight of me, halted, and stood there gazing straight towards us;—he was so close that I could see the firelight reflected in his wicked, greenish eyes.

"'Shoot, shoot!' said Mashune. 'The devil is coming—he is going to spring!'

"I raised the rifle, and got the bit of paper on the foresight, straight on to a little path of white hair just where the throat is set into the chest and shoulders. As I did so, the lion glanced back over his shoulder, as, according to my experience, a lion nearly always does before he springs. Then he dropped his body a little, and I saw his big paws spread out upon the ground as he put his weight on them to gather purchase. In haste I pressed the trigger of the Martini, and not a moment too soon; for, as I did so, he was in the act of springing. The report of the rifle rang out sharp and clear on the intense silence of the night, and in another second the great brute had landed on his head within four feet of us, and rolling over and over towards us, was sending the bushes which composed our little fence flying with convulsive strokes of his great paws. We sprang out of the other side of the 'skerm,' and he rolled on to it and into it and then right through the fire. Next he raised himself and sat upon his haunches like a great dog, and began to roar. Heavens! How he roared! I never heard anything like it before or since. He kept filling his lungs with air, and then emitting it in the most heart-shaking volumes of sound. Suddenly, in the middle of one of the loudest roars, he rolled over on to his side and lay still, and I knew that he was dead. A lion generally dies upon his side.

"With a sigh of relief I looked up towards his mate upon the ant-heap. She was standing there apparently petrified with astonishment, looking over her shoulder, and lashing her tail; but to our intense joy, when the dying beast ceased roaring, she turned, and, with one enormous bound, vanished into the night.

"Then we advanced cautiously towards the prostrate brute, Mashune droning an improvised Zulu song as he went, about how Macumazahn, the hunter of hunters, whose eyes are open by night as well as by day, put his hand down the lion's stomach when it came to devour him and pulled out his heart by the roots, &c., &c., by way of expressing his satisfaction, in his hyperbolical Zulu way, at the turn events had taken.

"There was no need for caution; the lion was as dead as though he had already been stuffed with straw. The Martini bullet had entered within an inch of the white spot I had aimed at, and travelled right through him, passing out at the right but-tock, near the root of the tail. The Martini has wonderful driving power, though the shock it gives to the system is, comparatively speaking, slight, owing to the smallness of the hole it makes. But fortunately the lion is an easy beast to kill.

"I passed the rest of that night in a profound slumber, my head reposing upon the deceased lion's flank, a position that had, I thought, a beautiful touch of irony about it, though the smell of his singed hair was disagreeable. When I woke again the faint primrose lights of dawn were flushing in the eastern sky. For a moment I could not understand the chill sense of anxiety that lay like a lump of ice at my heart, till the feel and smell of the skin of the dead lion beneath my head recalled the circumstances in which we were placed. I rose, and eagerly looked round to see if I could discover any signs of Hans, who, if he had escaped acci-dent, would surely return to us at dawn, but there were none. Then hope grew faint, and I felt that it was not well with the poor fellow. Setting Mashune to build up the fire I hastily removed the hide from the flank of the lion, which was indeed a splendid beast, and cutting off some lumps of flesh, we toasted and ate them greedily. Lions' flesh, strange as it may seem, is very good eating, and tastes more like veal than anything else.

"By the time we had finished our much-needed meal the sun was getting up, and after a drink of water and a wash at the pool, we started to try and find Hans, leaving the dead lion to the ten-der mercies of the hyænas. Both Mashune and myself were, by constant practice, pretty good hands at tracking, and we had not much difficulty in following the Hottentot's spoor, faint as it was. We had gone on in this way for half-an-hour or so, and were, per-haps, a mile or more from the site of our camping-place, when we discovered the spoor of a solitary bull buffalo mixed up with the spoor of Hans, and were able, from various indications, to make out that he had been tracking the buffalo. At length we reached a little glade in which there grew a stunted old mimosa thorn, with a peculiar and overhanging formation of root, under which a por-cupine, or an ant-bear, or some such animal, had hollowed out a wide-lipped hole. About ten or fifteen paces from this thorn-tree there was a thick patch of bush.

"'See, Macumazahn! See!' said Mashune, excitedly, as we drew near the thorn; 'the buffalo has charged him. Look, here he stood to fire at him; see how firmly he planted his feet upon the earth; there is the mark of his crooked toe (Hans had one bent toe). Look! Here the bull came like a boulder down the hill, his hoofs turning up the earth like a hoe. Hans had hit him: he bled as he came; there are the blood spots. It is all written down there, my father—there upon the earth.'

"'Yes,' I said; 'yes; but *where is Hans?*'

"Even as I said it Mashune clutched my arm, and pointed to the stunted thorn just by us. Even now, gentlemen, it makes me feel sick when I think of what I saw.

"For fixed in a stout fork of the tree some eight feet from the ground was Hans himself, or rather his dead body, evidently tossed there by the furious buffalo. One leg was twisted round the fork, probably in a dying convulsion. In the side, just beneath the ribs, was a great hole, from which the entrails protruded. But this was not all. The other leg hung down to within five feet of the ground. The skin and most of the flesh were gone from it. For a moment we stood aghast, and gazed at this horrifying sight. Then I understood what had happened. The buffalo, with that devilish cruelty which distinguishes the animal, had, after his enemy was dead, stood underneath his body, and licked the flesh off the pendant leg with his file-like tongue. I had heard of such a thing before, but had always treated the stories as hunters' yarns; but I had no doubt about it now. Poor Hans' skeleton foot and ankle were an ample proof.

"We stood aghast under the tree, and stared and stared at this awful sight, when suddenly our cogitations were interrupted in a painful manner. The thick bush about fifteen paces off burst asunder with a crashing sound, and uttering a series of ferocious pig-like grunts, the bull buffalo himself came charging out straight at us. Even as he came I saw the blood mark on his side where poor Hans' bullet had struck him, and also, as is often the case with particularly savage buffaloes, that his flanks had recently been terribly torn in an encounter with a lion.

"On he came, his head well up (a buffalo does not generally lower his head till he does so to strike); those great black horns—as I look at them before me, gentlemen, I seem to see them come charging at me as I did ten years ago, silhouetted against the green bush behind;—on, on!"

"With a shout Mashune bolted off sideways towards the bush. I had instinctively lifted my eight-bore, which I had in my hand. It would have been useless to fire at the buffalo's head, for the dense horns must have turned the bullet; but as Mashune bolted, the bull slewed a little, with the momentary idea of following him, and as this gave me a ghost of a chance, I let drive my only cartridge at his shoulder. The bullet struck the shoulder-blade and smashed it up, and then travelled on under the skin into his flank; but it did not stop him, though for a second he staggered.

"Throwing myself on to the ground with the energy of despair, I rolled under the shelter of the projecting root of the thorn, crushing myself as far into the mouth of the ant-bear hole as I could. In a single instant the buffalo was after me. Kneeling down on his uninjured knee —for one leg, that of which I had broken the shoulder, was swinging helplessly to and fro—he set to work to try and hook me out of the hole with his crooked horn. At first he struck at me furiously, and it was one of the blows against the base of the tree which splintered the tip of the horn in the way that you see. Then he grew more cunning, and pushed his head as far under the root as possible, made long semicircular sweeps at me, grunting furiously, and blowing saliva and hot steamy breath all over me. I was just out of reach of the horn, though every stroke, by widening the hole and making more room for his head, brought it closer to me, but every now and again I received heavy blows in the ribs from his muzzle. Feeling that I was being knocked silly, I made an effort and seizing his rough tongue, which was hanging from his jaws, I twisted it with all my force. The great brute bellowed with pain and fury, and jerked himself backwards so strongly, that he dragged me some inches further from the mouth of the hole, and again made a sweep at me, catching me this time round the shoulder-joint in the hook of his horn.

"I felt that it was all up now, and began to holloa.

"'He has got me!' I shouted in mortal terror. '*Gwasa, Mashune, gwasa!*' ('Stab, Mashune, stab!').

"One hoist of the great head, and out of the hole I came like a periwinkle out of his shell. But even as I did so, I caught sight of Mashune's stalwart form advancing with his 'bangwan,' or broad stabbing assegai, raised above his head. In another quarter of a second I had fallen from the horn, and heard the blow of the spear, followed by the indescribable sound of steel shearing its way through flesh. I had fallen on my back, and, looking up, I saw that the gallant Mashune had driven the assegai a foot or more into the carcass of the buffalo, and was turning to fly.

"Alas! It was too late. Bellowing madly, and spouting blood from mouth and nostrils, the devilish brute was on him, and had thrown him up like a feather, and then gored him twice as he lay. I struggled up with some wild idea of affording help, but before I had gone a step the buffalo gave one long sighing bellow, and rolled over dead by the side of his victim.

"Mashune was still living, but a single glance at him told me that his hour had come. The buffalo's horn had driven a great hole in his right lung, and inflicted other injuries.

"I knelt down beside him in the uttermost distress, and took his hand.

"'Is he dead, Macumazahn?' he whispered. 'My eyes are blind; I cannot see.'

"'Yes, he is dead.'

"'Did the black devil hurt thee, Macumazahn?'

"'No, my poor fellow, I am not much hurt.'

"'Ow! I am glad.'

"Then came a long silence, broken only by the sound of the air whistling through the hole in his lung as he breathed.

"'Macumazahn, art thou there? I cannot feel thee.'

"'I am here, Mashune.'

"'I die, Macumazahn—the world flies round and round. I go—I go out into the dark! Surely, my father, at times in days to come—thou wilt think of Mashune who stood by thy side—when thou killest elephants, as we used—as we used—'

"They were his last words, his brave spirit passed with him. I dragged his body to the hole under the tree, and pushed it in, placing his broad assegai by him, according to the custom of his people, that he might not go defenceless on his long journey; and then, ladies—I am not ashamed to confess—I stood alone there before it, and wept like a woman."

A TALE OF THREE LIONS

CHAPTER I

THE INTEREST ON TEN SHILLINGS

Most of you will have heard that Allan Quatermain, who was one of the party that discovered King Solomon's mines some little time ago, and who afterwards came to live in England near his friend Sir Henry Curtis. He went back to the wilderness again, as these old hunters almost invariably do, on one pretext or another.[2] They cannot endure civilization for very long, its noise and racket and the omnipresence of broadclothed humanity proving more trying to their nerves than the dangers of the desert. I think that they feel lonely here, for it is a fact that is too little understood, though it has often been stated, that there is no loneliness like the loneliness of crowds, especially to those who are unaccustomed to them. "What is there in the world," old Quatermain would say, "so desolate as to stand in the streets of a great city and listen to the footsteps falling, falling, multitudinous as the rain, and watch the white line of faces as they hurry past, you know not whence, you know not whither? They come and go, their eyes meet yours with a cold stare, for a moment their features are written on your mind, and then they are gone for ever. You will never see them again; they will never see you again; they come up out of the unknown, and presently they once more vanish into the unknown, taking their secrets with them. Yes, that is loneliness pure and undefiled; but to one who knows and loves it, the wilderness is

---

2 This of course was written before Mr. Quatermain's account of the adventures in the newly-discovered country of Zu-Vendis of himself, Sir Henry Curtis, and Capt. John Good had been received in England.—Editor.

not lonely, because the spirit of nature is ever there to keep the wanderer company. He finds companions in the winds—the sunny streams babble like Nature's children at his feet; high above them, in the purple sunset, are domes and minarets and palaces, such as no mortal man has built, in and out of whose flaming doors the angels of the sun seem to move continually. And there, too, is the wild game, following its feeding-grounds in great armies, with the springbuck thrown out before for skirmishers; then rank upon rank of long-faced blesbuck, marching and wheeling like infantry; and last the shining troops of quagga, and the fierce-eyed shaggy vilderbeeste to take, as it were, the place of the cossack host that hangs upon an army's flanks.

"Oh, no," he would say, "the wilderness is not lonely, for, my boy, remember that the further you get from man, the nearer you grow to God," and though this is a saying that might well be disputed, it is one I am sure that anybody will easily understand who has watched the sun rise and set on the limitless deserted plains, and seen the thunder chariots of the clouds roll in majesty across the depths of unfathomable sky.

Well, at any rate we went back again, and now for many months I have heard nothing at all of him, and to be frank, I greatly doubt if anybody will ever hear of him again. I fear that the wilderness, that has for so many years been a mother to him, will now also prove his grave and the grave of those who accompanied him, for the quest upon which he and they have started is a wild one indeed.

But while he was in England for those three years or so between his return from the successful discovery of the wise king's buried treasures, and the death of his only son, I saw a great deal of old Allan Quatermain. I had known him years before in Africa, and after he came home, whenever I had nothing better to do, I used to run up to Yorkshire and stay with him, and in this way I at one time and another heard many of the incidents of his past life, and most curious some of them were. No man can pass all those years following the rough existence of an elephant-hunter without meeting with many strange adventures, and in one way and another old Quatermain has certainly seen his share. Well, the story that I am going to tell you in the following pages is one of the later of these adventures, though I forget the exact year in which it happened. at any rate I know that it was the only trip upon which he took his son Harry (who is since dead) with him, and that Harry was then about fourteen. And now for the story, which I will repeat, as nearly as I can, in the words in which Hunter Quatermain told it to me one night in the old oak-panelled vestibule of his house in Yorkshire. We were talking about gold-mining—

"Gold-mining!" he broke in. "Ah! Yes, I once went gold-mining at Pilgrims' Rest in the Transvaal, and it was after that that we had the business about Jim-Jim and the lions. Do you know Pilgrim's Rest? Well, it is, or was, one of the queerest little places you ever saw. The town itself was pitched in a stony valley, with mountains all about it, and in the middle of such scenery as one does not often get the chance of seeing. Many and many is the time that I have thrown down my pick and shovel in disgust, clambered out of my claim, and walked a couple of miles or so to the top of some hill. Then I would lie down in the grass and look out over the glorious stretch of country—the smiling valleys, the great mountains touched with gold— real gold of the sunset, and clothed in sweeping robes of bush, and stare into the depths of the perfect sky above; yes, and thank Heaven I had got away from the cursing and the coarse jokes of the miners, and the voices of those Basutu Kaffirs as they toiled in the sun, the memory of which is with me yet.

"Well, for some months I dug away patiently at my claim, till the very sight of a pick or of a washing-trough became hateful to me. A hundred times a day I lamented my own folly in having invested eight hundred pounds, which was about all that I was worth at the time, in this gold-mining. But like other better people before me, I had been bitten by the gold bug, and now was forced to take the consequences. I bought a claim out of which a man had made a fortune—five or six thousand pounds at least—as I thought, very cheap; that is, I gave him five hundred pounds down for it. It was all that I had made by a very rough year's elephant-hunting beyond the Zambesi, and I sighed deeply and prophetically when I saw my successful friend, who was a Yankee, sweep up the roll of Standard Bank notes with the lordly air of the man who has made his fortune, and cram them into his breeches pockets. 'Well,' I said to him—the happy vendor—'it is a magnificent property, and I only hope that my luck will be as good as yours has been.'

"He smiled; to my excited nerves it seemed that he smiled ominously, as he answered me in a peculiar Yankee drawl: 'I guess, stranger, as I ain't the one to make a man quarrel with his food, more especial when there ain't no more going of the rounds; and as for that there claim, well, she's been a good nigger to me; but between you and me, stranger, speaking man to man, now that there ain't any filthy lucre between us to obscure the features of the truth, I guess she's about worked out!'

"I gasped; the fellow's effrontery took the breath out of me. Only five minutes before he had been swearing by all his gods—and they appeared to be numerous and mixed—that there were half a dozen fortunes left in the claim, and that he was only giving it up because he was downright weary of shovelling the gold out.

"'Don't look so vexed, stranger,' went on my tormentor, 'perhaps there is some shine in the old girl yet; anyway you are a downright good fellow, you are, therefore you will, I guess, have a real A1 opportunity of working on the feelings of Fortune. Anyway it will bring the muscle up upon your arm, for the stuff is uncommon stiff, and, what is more, you will in the course of a year earn a sight more than two thousand dollars in value of experience.'

"Then he went just in time, for in another moment I should have gone for him, and I saw his face no more.

"Well, I set to work on the old claim with my boy Harry and half a dozen Kaffirs to help me, which, seeing that I had put nearly all my worldly wealth into it, was the least that I could do. And we worked, my word, we did work—early and late we went at it—but never a bit of gold did we see; no, not even a nugget large enough to make a scarf-pin out of. The American gentleman had secured it all and left us the sweepings.

"For three months this went on, till at last I had paid away all, or very near all, that was left of her little capital in wages and food for the Kaffirs and ourselves. When I tell you that Boer meal was sometimes as high as four pounds a bag, you will understand that it did not take long to run through our banking account.

"At last the crisis came. One Saturday night I had paid the men as usual, and bought a muid of mealie meal at sixty shillings for them to fill themselves with, and then I went with my boy Harry and sat on the edge of the great hole that we had dug in the hill-side, and which we had in bitter mockery named Eldorado. There we sat in the moonlight with our feet over the edge of the claim, and were melancholy enough for anything. Presently I pulled out my purse and emptied its contents into my hand. There was a half-sovereign, two florins, ninepence in silver, no coppers—for copper practically does not circulate in South Africa, which is one of the things that make living so dear there—in all exactly fourteen and ninepence.

"'There, Harry, my boy!' I said, 'that is the sum total of our worldly wealth; that hole has swallowed all the rest.'

"'By George!' said Master Harry; 'I say, father, you and I shall have to let ourselves out to work with the Kaffirs and live on mealie pap,' and he sniggered at his unpleasant little joke.

"But I was in no mood for joking, for it is not a merry thing to dig like anything for months and be completely ruined in the process, especially if you happen to dislike digging, and consequently I resented Harry's light-heartedness.

"'Be quiet, boy!' I said, raising my hand as though to give him a cuff, with the result that the half-sovereign slipped out of it and fell into the gulf below.

"'Oh, bother,' said I, 'it's gone.'

"'There, Dad,' said Harry, 'that's what comes of letting your angry passions rise; now we are down to four and nine.'

"I made no answer to these words of wisdom, but scrambled down the steep sides of the claim, followed by Harry, to hunt for my little all. Well, we hunted and we hunted, but the moonlight is an uncertain thing to look for half-sovereigns by, and there was some loose soil about, for the Kaffirs had knocked off working at this very spot a couple of hours before. I took a pick and raked away the clods of earth with it, in the hope of finding the coin; but all in vain. At last in sheer annoyance I struck the sharp end of the pickaxe down into the soil, which was of a very hard nature. To my astonishment it sunk in right up to the haft.

"'Why, Harry,' I said, 'this ground must have been disturbed!'

"'I don't think so, father,' he answered; 'but we will soon see,' and he began to shovel out the soil with his hands. 'Oh,' he said presently, 'it's only some old stones; the pick has gone down between them, look!' and he began to pull at one of the stones.

"'I say, Dad,' he said presently, almost in a whisper, 'it's precious heavy, feel it;' and he rose and gave me a round, brownish lump about the size of a very large apple, which he was holding in both his hands. I took it curiously and held it up to the light. It *was* very heavy. The moonlight fell upon its rough and filth-encrusted surface, and as I looked, curious little thrills of excitement began to pass through me. But I could not be sure.

"'Give me your knife, Harry,' I said.

"He did so, and resting the brown stone on my knee I scratched at its surface. Great heavens, it was soft!

"Another second and the secret was out, we had found a great nugget of pure gold, four pounds of it or more. 'It's gold, lad,' I said, 'it's gold, or I'm a Dutchman!'

"Harry, with his eyes starting out of his head, glared down at the gleaming yellow scratch that I had made upon the virgin metal, and then burst out into yell upon yell of exultation, which went ringing away across the silent claims like shrieks of somebody being murdered.

"'Be quiet!' I said; 'do you want every thief on the fields after you?'

"Scarcely were the words out of my mouth when I heard a stealthy footstep approaching. I promptly put the big nugget down and sat on it, and uncommonly hard it was. As I did so I saw a lean dark face poked over the edge of the claim and a pair of beady eyes searching us out. I knew the face, it belonged to a man of very bad character known as Handspike Tom, who had, I understood, been so named at the Diamond Fields because he had murdered his mate with a handspike. He was now no doubt prowling about like a human hyæna to see what he could steal.

"'Is that you, 'Unter Quatermain?' he said.

"'Yes, it's I, Mr. Tom,' I answered, politely.

"'And what might all that there yelling be?' he asked. 'I was walking along, a-taking of the evening air and a-thinking on the stars, when I 'ears 'owl after 'owl.'

"'Well, Mr. Tom,' I answered, 'that is not to be wondered at, seeing that like yourself they are nocturnal birds.'

"''Owl after 'owl!' he repeated sternly, taking no notice of my interpretation, 'and I stops and says, "That's murder," and I listens again and thinks, "No, it ain't; that 'owl is the 'owl of hexultation; someone's been and got his fingers into a gummy yeller pot, I'll swear, and gone off 'is 'ead in the sucking of them." Now, 'Unter Quatermain, is I right? Is it nuggets? Oh, lor!' and he smacked his lips audibly—'great big yellow boys—is it them that you have just been and tumbled across?'

"'No,' I said boldly, 'it isn't'—the cruel gleam in his black eyes altogether overcoming my aversion to untruth, for I knew that if once he found out what it was that I was sitting on—and by the way I have heard of rolling in gold being spoken of as a pleasant process, but I certainly do not recommend anybody who values comfort to try sitting on it—I should run a very good chance of being 'handspiked' before the night was over.

"'If you want to know what it was, Mr. Tom,' I went on, with my politest air, although in agony from the nugget under-neath—for I hold it is always best to be polite to a man who is so ready with a handspike—'my boy and I have had a slight differ-ence of opinion, and I was enforcing my view of the matter upon him; that's all.'

"'Yes, Mr. Tom,' put in Harry, beginning to weep, for Harry was a smart boy, and saw the difficulty we were in, 'that was it—I halloed because father beat me.'

"'Well, now, did yer, my dear boy—did yer? Well, all I can say is that a played-out old claim is a wonderful queer sort of place to come to for to argify at ten o'clock of night, and what's more, my sweet youth, if ever I should 'ave the argifying of yer'—and he leered unpleasantly at Harry—'yer won't 'oller in quite such a jolly sort o' way. And now I'll be saying good-night, for I don't like disturbing of a family party. No, I ain't that sort of man, I ain't. Good-night to yer, 'Unter Quatermain—good-night to yer, my argified young one;' and Mr. Tom turned away disappointed, and prowled off elsewhere, like a human jackal, to see what he could thieve or kill.

"'Thank goodness!' I said, as I slipped off the lump of gold. 'Now, then, do you get up, Harry, and see if that consummate villain has gone.' Harry did so, and reported that he had vanished towards Pilgrim's Rest, and then we set to work, and very carefully, but trembling with excitement, with our hands hollowed out all the space of ground into which I had struck the pick. Yes, as I hoped, there was a regular nest of nuggets, twelve in all, running from the size of a hazel-nut to that of a hen's egg, though of course the first one was much larger than that. How they all came there nobody can say; it was one of those extraordinary freaks, with stories of which, at any rate, all people acquainted with alluvial gold-mining will be familiar. It turned out afterwards that the American who sold me the claim had in the same way made his pile—a much larger one than ours, by the way— out of a single pocket, and then worked for six months without seeing colour, after which he gave it up.

"At any rate, there the nuggets were, to the value, as it turned out afterwards, of about twelve hundred and fifty pounds, so that after all I took out of that hole four hundred and fifty pounds more than I put into it. We got them all out and wrapped them up in a handkerchief, and then, fearing to carry home so much treasure, especially as we knew that Mr. Handspike Tom was on the prowl, made up our minds to pass the night where we were—a necessity which, disagreeable as it was, was wonderfully sweetened by the presence of that handkerchief full of virgin gold—the interest of my lost half-sovereign.

"Slowly the night wore away, for with the fear of Handspike Tom before my eyes I did not dare to go to sleep, and at last the dawn came. I got up and watched its growth, till it opened like a flower upon the eastern sky, and the sunbeams began to spring up in splendour from mountain-top to mountain-top. I watched it, and as I did so it flashed upon me, with a complete conviction which I had not felt before, that I had had enough of gold-mining to last me the rest of my natural life, and I then and there made up my mind to clear out of Pilgrims' Rest and go and shoot buffalo towards Delagoa Bay. Then I turned, took the pick and shovel, and although it was a Sunday morning, woke up Harry and set to work to see if there were any more nuggets about. As I expected, there were none. What we had got had lain together in a little pocket filled with soil that felt quite different from the stiff stuff round and outside the pocket. There was not another trace of gold. Of course it is possible that there were more pocketfuls somewhere about, but all I have to say is I made up my mind that, whoever found them, I should not; and, as a matter of fact, I have since heard that this claim has been the ruin of two or three people, as it very nearly was the ruin of me.

"'Harry,' I said presently, 'I am going away this week towards Delagoa to shoot buffalo. Shall I take you with me, or send you down to Durban?'

"'Oh, take me with you, father!' begged Harry, 'I want to kill a buffalo!'

"'And supposing that the buffalo kills you instead?' I asked.

"'Oh, never mind,' he said, gaily, 'there are lots more where I came from.'

"I rebuked him for his flippancy, but in the end I consented to take him.

CHAPTER II

WHAT WAS FOUND IN THE POOL

"Something over a fortnight had passed since the night when I lost half-a-sovereign and found twelve hundred and fifty pounds in looking for it, and instead of that horrid hole, for which, after all, Eldorado was hardly a misnomer, a very different scene stretched away before us clad in the silver robe of the moonlight. We were camped— Harry and I, two Kaffirs, a Scotch cart, and six oxen—on the swelling side of a great wave of bushclad land. Just where we had made our camp, however, the bush was very sparse, and only grew about in clumps, while here and there were single flat-topped mimosa-trees. To our right a little stream, which had cut a deep channel for itself in the bosom of the slope, flowed musically on between banks green with maidenhair, wild asparagus, and many beautiful grasses. The bed-rock here was red granite, and in the course of centuries of patient washing the water had hollowed out some of the huge slabs in its path into great troughs and cups, and these we used for bathing-places. No Roman lady, with her baths of porphyry or alabaster, could have had a more delicious spot to bathe herself than we found within fifty yards of our skerm, or rough inclosure of mimosa thorn, that we had dragged together round the cart to protect us from the attacks of lions. That there were several of these brutes about, I knew from their spoor, though we had neither heard nor seen them.

"Our bath was a little nook where the eddy of the stream had washed away a mass of soil, and on the edge of it there grew a most beautiful old mimosa thorn. Beneath the thorn was a large smooth slab of granite fringed all round with maidenhair and other ferns, that sloped gently down to a pool of the clearest sparkling water, which lay in a bowl of granite about ten feet wide by five feet deep in the centre. Here to this slab we went every morning to bathe, and that delightful bath is among the most pleasant of my hunting reminiscences, as it is also, for reasons which will presently appear, among the most painful.

"It was a lovely night. Harry and I sat to the windward of the fire, where the two Kaffirs were busily employed in cooking some impala steaks off a buck which Harry, to his great joy, had shot that morning, and were as perfectly contented with ourselves and the world at large as two people could possibly be. The night was beautiful, and it would require somebody with more words on the tip of his tongue than I have to describe properly the chastened majesty of those moonlit wilds. Away for ever and for ever, away to the mysterious north, rolled the great bush ocean over which the silence brooded. There beneath us a mile or more to the right ran the wide Oliphant, and mirror-like flashed back the moon, whose silver spears were shivered on its breast, and then tossed in twisted lines of light far and wide about the mountains and the plain. Down upon the river-banks grew great timber-trees that through the stillness pointed solemnly to Heaven, and the beauty of the night lay upon them like a cloud. Everywhere was silence—silence in the starred depths, silence on the bosom of the sleeping earth. Now, if ever, great thoughts might rise in a man's mind, and for a space he might forget his littleness in the sense that he partook of the pure immensity about him.

"'Hark! What was that?'

"From far away down by the river there comes a mighty rolling sound, then another, and another. It is the lion seeking his meat.

"I saw Harry shiver and turn a little pale. He was a plucky boy enough, but the roar of a lion heard for the first time in the solemn bush veldt at night is apt to shake the nerves of any lad.

"'Lions, my boy,' I said; 'they are hunting down by the river there; but I don't think that you need make yourself uneasy. We have been here three nights now, and if they were going to pay us a visit I think that they would have done so before this. However, we will make up the fire.'

"'Here, Pharaoh, do you and Jim-Jim get some more wood before we go to sleep, else the cats will be purring round you before morning.'

"Pharaoh, a great brawny Swazi, who had been working for me at Pilgrims' Rest, laughed, rose, and stretched himself, then calling to Jim-Jim to bring the axe and a reim, started off in the moonlight towards a clump of sugar-bush where we cut our fuel from some dead trees. He was a fine fellow in his way, was Pharaoh, and I think that he had been named Pharaoh because he had an Egyptian cast of countenance and a royal sort of swagger about him. But his way was a somewhat peculiar way, on account of the uncertainty of his temper, and very few people could get on with him; also if he could find liquor he would drink like a fish, and when he drank he became shockingly bloodthirsty. These were his bad points; his good ones were that, like most people of the Zulu blood, he became exceedingly attached if he took to you at all; he was a hard-working and intelligent man, and about as dare-devil and plucky a fellow at a pinch as I have ever had to do with. He was about five-and-thirty years of age or so, but not a 'keshla' or ringed man. I believe that he had got into trouble in some way in Swaziland, and the authorities of his tribe would not allow him to assume the ring, and that is why he came to work at the gold-fields. The other man, or rather lad, Jim-Jim, was a Mapoch Kaffir, or Knobnose, and even in the light of subsequent events I fear I cannot speak very well of him. He was an idle and careless young rascal, and only that very morning I had to tell Pharaoh to give him a beating for letting the oxen stray, which Pharaoh did with the greatest gusto, although he was by way of being very fond of Jim-Jim. Indeed, I saw him consoling Jim-Jim afterwards with a pinch of snuff from his own ear-box, whilst he explained to him that the next time it came in the way of duty to flog him, he meant to thrash him with the other hand, so as to cross the old cuts and make a "pretty pattern" on his back.

"Well, off they went, though Jim-Jim did not at all like leaving the camp at that hour, even when the moonlight was so bright, and in due course returned safely enough with a great bundle of wood. I laughed at Jim-Jim, and asked him if he had seen anything, and he said yes, he had; he had seen two large yellow eyes staring at him from behind a bush, and heard something snore.

"As, however, on further investigation the yellow eyes and the snore appeared to have existed only in Jim-Jim's lively imagination, I was not greatly disturbed by this alarming report; but having seen to the making-up of the fire, got into the skerm and went quietly to sleep with Harry by my side.

"Some hours afterwards I woke up with a start. I don't know what woke me. The moon had gone down, or at least was almost hidden behind the soft horizon of bush, only her red rim being visible. Also a wind had sprung up and was driving long hurrying lines of cloud across the starry sky, and altogether a great change had come over the mood of the night. By the look of the sky I judged that we must be about two hours from daybreak.

"The oxen, which were as usual tied to the disselboom of the Scotch cart, were very restless—they kept snuffling and blowing, and rising up and lying down again, so I at once suspected that they must wind something. Presently I knew what it was that they winded, for within fifty yards of us a lion roared, not very loud, but quite loud enough to make my heart come into my mouth.

"Pharaoh was sleeping on the other side of the cart, and, looking beneath it, I saw him raise his head and listen.

"'Lion, Inkoos,' he whispered, 'lion!'

"Jim-Jim also jumped up, and by the faint light I could see that he was in a very great fright indeed.

"Thinking that it was as well to be prepared for emergencies, I told Pharaoh to throw wood upon the fire, and woke up Harry, who I verily believe was capable of sleeping happily through the crack of doom. He was a little scared at first, but presently the excitement of the position came home to him, and he grew quite anxious to see his majesty face to face. I got my rifle handy and gave Harry his—a Westley Richards falling block, which is a very useful gun for a youth, being light and yet a good killing rifle, and then we waited.

"For a long time nothing happened, and I began to think that the best thing we could do would be to go to sleep again, when suddenly I heard a sound more like a cough than a roar within about twenty yards of the skerm. We all looked out, but could see nothing; and then followed another period of suspense. It was very trying to the nerves, this waiting for an attack that might be developed from any quarter or might not be developed at all; and though I was an old hand at this sort of business I was anxious about Harry, for it is wonderful how the presence of anybody to whom one is attached unnerves a man in moments of danger. I know, although it was now chilly enough, I could feel the perspiration running down my nose, and in order to relieve the strain on my attention employed myself in watching a beetle which appeared to be attracted by the firelight, and was sitting before it thoughtfully rubbing his antennæ against each other.

"Suddenly, the beetle gave such a jump that he nearly pitched headlong into the fire, and so did we all—gave jumps, I mean, and no wonder, for from right under the skerm fence there came a most frightful roar —a roar that literally made the Scotch cart shake and took the breath out of me.

"Harry made an exclamation, Jim-Jim howled outright, while the poor oxen, who were terrified almost out of their hides, shivered and lowed piteously.

"The night was almost entirely dark now, for the moon had quite set, and the clouds had covered up the stars, so that the only light we had came from the fire, which by this time was burning up brightly again. But, as you know, firelight is absolutely useless to shoot by, it is so uncertain, and besides, it penetrates but a very little way into the darkness, although if one is in the dark outside, one can see it from far away.

"Presently the oxen, after standing still for a moment, suddenly winded the lion and did what I feared they would do—began to 'skrek,' that is, to try and break loose from the trektow to which they were tied, to rush off madly into the wilderness. Lions know of this habit on the part of oxen, which are, I do believe, the most foolish animals under the sun, a sheep being a very Solomon compared to them; and it is by no means uncommon for a lion to get in such a position that a herd or span of oxen may wind him, skrek, break their reims, and rush off into the bush. Of course, once there, they are helpless in the dark; and then the lion chooses the one that he loves best and eats him at his leisure.

"Well, round and round went our six poor oxen, nearly trampling us to death in their mad rush; indeed, had we not hastily tumbled out of the way, we should have been trodden to death, or at the least seriously injured. As it was, Harry was run over, and poor Jim-Jim being caught by the trektow somewhere beneath the arm, was hurled right across the skerm, landing by my side only some paces off.

"Snap went the disselboom of the cart beneath the transverse strain put upon it. Had it not broken the cart would have overset; as it was, in another minute, oxen, cart, trektow, reims, broken disselboom, and everything were soon tied in one vast heaving, plunging, bellowing, and seemingly inextricable knot.

"For a moment or two this state of affairs took my attention off from the lion that had caused it, but whilst I was wondering what on earth was to be done next, and how we should manage if the cattle broke loose into the bush and were lost—for cattle frightened in this manner will so straight away like mad things—my thoughts were suddenly recalled to the lion in a very painful fashion.

"For at that moment I perceived by the light of the fire a kind of gleam of yellow travelling through the air towards us.

"'The lion! The lion!' holloaed Pharaoh, and as he did so, he, or rather she, for it was a great gaunt lioness, half wild no doubt with hunger, lit right in the middle of the skerm, and stood there in the smoky gloom lashing her tail and roaring. I seized my rifle and fired it at her, but what between the confusion, my agitation, and the uncertain light, I missed her, and nearly shot Pharaoh. The flash of the rifle, however, threw the whole scene into strong relief, and a wild sight it was I can tell you—with the seething mass of oxen twisted all round the cart, in such a fashion that their heads looked as though they were growing out of their rumps; and their horns seemed to protrude from their backs; the smoking fire with just a blaze in the heart of the smoke; Jim-Jim in the foreground, where the oxen had thrown him in their wild rush, stretched out there in terror, and then as a centre to the picture the great gaunt lioness glaring round with hungry yellow eyes, roaring and whining as she made up her mind what to do.

"It did not take her long, however, just the time that it takes a flash to die into darkness, for, before I could fire again or do anything, with a most fiendish snort she sprang upon poor Jim-Jim.

"I heard the unfortunate lad shriek, and then almost instantly I saw his legs thrown into the air. The lioness had seized him by the neck, and with a sudden jerk thrown his body over her back so that his legs hung down upon the further side.[3] Then, without the slightest hesitation, and apparently without any difficulty, she cleared the skerm face at a single bound, and bearing poor Jim-Jim with her vanished into the darkness beyond, in the direction of the bathing-place that I have already described. We jumped up perfectly mad with horror and fear, and rushed wildly after her, firing shots at haphazard on the chance that she would be frightened by them into dropping her prey, but nothing could we see, and nothing could we hear. The lioness had vanished into the darkness, taking Jim-Jim with her, and to attempt to follow her till daylight was madness. We should only expose ourselves to the risk of a like fate.

"So with scared and heavy hearts we crept back to the skerm, and sat down to wait for the dawn, which now could not

3   I have known a lion carry a two-year-old ox over a stone wall four feet high in this fashion, and a mile away into the bush beyond. He was subsequently poisoned by strychnine put into the carcass of the ox, and I still have his claws.—Editor.

be much more than an hour off. It was absolutely useless to try even to disentangle the oxen till then, so all that was left for us to do was to sit and wonder how it came to pass that the one should be taken and the other left, and to hope against hope that our poor servant might have been mercifully delivered from the lion's jaws.

"At length the faint dawn came stealing like a ghost up the long slope of bush, and glinted on the tangled oxen's horns, and with white and frightened faces we got up and set to the task of disentangling the oxen, till such time as there should be light enough to enable us to follow the trail of the lioness which had gone off with Jim-Jim. And here a fresh trouble awaited us, for when at last with infinite difficulty we had disentangled the great helpless brutes, it was only to find that one of the best of them was very sick. There was no mistake about the way he stood with his legs slightly apart and his head hanging down. He had got the redwater, I was sure of it. Of all the difficulties connected with life and travelling in South Africa those connected with oxen are perhaps the worst. The ox is the most exasperating animal in the world, a negro excepted. He has absolutely no constitution, and never neglects an opportunity of falling sick of some mysterious disease. He will get thin upon the slightest provocation, and from mere maliciousness die of 'poverty'; whereas it is his chief delight to turn round and refuse to pull whenever he finds himself well in the centre of a river, or the waggon-wheel nicely fast in a mud hole. Drive him a few miles over rough roads and you will find that he is footsore; turn him loose to feed and you will discover that he has run away, or if he has not run away he has of malice aforethought eaten 'tulip' and poisoned himself. There is always something with him. The ox is a brute. It was of a piece with his accustomed behaviour for the one in question to break out—on purpose probably—with redwater just when a lion had walked off with his herd. It was exactly what I should have expected, and I was therefore neither disappointed nor surprised.

"Well, it was no use crying as I should almost have liked to do, because if this ox had redwater it was probable that the rest of them had it too, although they had been sold to me as 'salted,' that is, proof against such diseases as redwater and lungsick. One gets hardened to this sort of thing in South Africa in course of time, for I suppose in no other country in the world is the waste of animal life so great.

"So taking my rifle and telling Harry to follow me (for we had to leave Pharaoh to look after the oxen—Pharaoh's lean kine, I called them), I started to see if anything could be found of or appertaining to the unfortunate Jim-Jim. The ground round our little camp was hard and rocky, and we could not hit off any spoor of the lioness, though just outside the skerm was a drop or two of blood. About three hundred yards from the camp, and a little to the right, was a patch of sugar bush mixed up with the usual mimosa, and for this I made, thinking that the lioness would have been sure to take her prey there to devour it. On we pushed through the long grass that was bent down beneath the weight of the soaking dew. In two minutes we were wet through up to the thighs, as wet as though we had waded through water. In due course, however, we reached the patch of bush, and by the grey light of the morning cautiously and slowly pushed our way into it. It was very dark under the trees, for the sun was not yet up, so we walked with the most extreme care, half expecting every minute to come across the lioness licking the bones of poor Jim-Jim. But no lioness could we see, and as for Jim-Jim there was not even a finger-joint of him to be found. Evidently they had not come here.

"So pushing through the bush we proceeded to hunt every other likely spot, but with the same result.

"'I suppose she must have taken him right away,' I said at last, sadly enough. 'At any rate he will be dead by now, so God have mercy on him, we can't help him. What's to be done now?'

"'I suppose that we had better wash ourselves in the pool, and then go back and get something to eat. I am filthy,' said Harry.

"This was a practical if a somewhat unfeeling suggestion. At least it struck me as unfeeling to talk of washing when poor Jim-Jim had been so recently eaten. However, I did not let my sentiment carry me away, so we went down to the beautiful spot that I have described, to wash. I was the first to reach it, which I did by scrambling down the ferny bank. Then I turned round, and started back with a yell—as well I might, for almost from beneath my feet there came a most awful snarl.

"I had lit nearly upon the back of the lioness, that had been sleeping on the slab where we always stood to dry ourselves after bathing. With a snarl and a growl, before I could do anything, before I could even cock my rifle, she had bounded right across the crystal pool, and vanished over the opposite bank. It was all done in an instant, as quick as thought.

"She had been sleeping on the slab, and oh, horror! What was that sleeping beside her? It was the red remains of poor Jim-Jim, lying on a patch of blood-stained rock.

"'Oh! Father, father!' shrieked Harry, 'look in the water!'

"I looked. There, floating in the centre of the lovely tranquil pool, was Jim-Jim's head. The lioness had bitten it right off, and it had rolled down the sloping rock into the water.

CHAPTER III

JIM-JIM IS AVENGED

"We never bathed in that pool again; indeed for my part I could never look at its peaceful purity fringed round with waving ferns without thinking of that ghastly head which rolled itself off through the water when we tried to catch it.

"Poor Jim-Jim! We buried what was left of him, which was not very much, in an old bread-bag, and though whilst he lived his virtues were not great, now that he was gone we could have wept over him. Indeed, Harry did weep outright; while Pharaoh used very bad language in Zulu, and I registered a quiet little vow on my account that I would let daylight into that lioness before I was forty-eight hours older, if by any means it could be done.

"Well, we buried him, and there he lies in the bread-bag (which I rather grudged him, as it was the only one we had), where lions will not trouble him any more—though perhaps the hyænas will, if they consider that there is enough on him left to make it worth their while to dig him up. However, he won't mind that; so there is an end of the book of Jim-Jim.

"The question that now remained was, how to circumvent his murderess. I knew that she would be sure to return as soon as she was hungry again, but I did not know when she would be hungry. She had left so little of Jim-Jim behind her that I should scarcely expect to see her the next night, unless indeed she had cubs. Still, I felt that it would not be wise to miss the chance of her coming, so we set about making preparations for her reception. The first thing that we did was to strengthen the bush wall of the skerm by dragging a large quantity of the tops of thorn-trees together, and laying them one on the other in such a fashion that the thorns pointed outwards. This, after our experience of the fate of Jim-Jim, seemed a very necessary precaution, since if where one goat can jump another can follow, as the Kaffirs say, how much more is this the case when an animal so active and so vigorous as the lion is concerned! And now came the further question, how were we to beguile the lioness to return? Lions are animals that have a strange knack of appearing when they are not wanted, and keeping studiously out of the way when their presence is required. Of course it was possible that if she had found Jim-Jim to her liking she would come back to see if there were any more of his kind about, but still it was not to be relied on.

"Harry, who as I have said was an eminently practical boy, suggested to Pharaoh that he should go and sit outside the skerm in the moonlight as a sort of bait, assuring him that he would have nothing to fear, as we should certainly kill the lioness before she killed him. Pharaoh however, strangely enough, did not seem to take to this suggestion. Indeed, he walked away, much put out with Harry for having made it.

"It gave me an idea, however.

"'By Jove!' I said, 'there is the sick ox. He must die sooner or later, so we may as well utilize him.'

"Now, about thirty yards to the left of our skerm, as one stood facing down the hill towards the river, was the stump of a tree that had been destroyed by lightning many years before, standing equidistant between, but a little in front of, two clumps of bush, which were severally some fifteen paces from it.

"Here was the very place to tie the ox; and accordingly a little before sunset the sick animal was led forth by Pharaoh and made fast there, little knowing, poor brute, for what purpose; and we began our long vigil, this time without a fire, for our object was to attract the lioness and not to scare her.

"For hour after hour we waited, keeping ourselves awake by pinching each other—it is, by the way, remarkable what a difference of opinion as to the force of pinches requisite to the occasion exists in the mind of pincher and pinched—but no lioness came. At last the moon went down, and darkness swallowed up the world, as the Kaffirs say, but no lions came to swallow us up. We waited till dawn, because we did not dare to go to sleep, and then at last with many bad thoughts in our hearts we took such rest as we could get, and that was not much.

"That morning we went out shooting, not because we wanted to, for we were too depressed and tired, but because we had no more meat. For three hours or more we wandered about in a broiling sun looking for something to kill, but with absolutely no results. For some unknown reason the game had grown very scarce about the spot, though when I was there two years before every sort of large game except rhinoceros and elephant was particularly abundant. The lions, of whom there were many, alone remained, and I fancy that it was the fact of the game they live on having temporarily migrated which made them so daring and ferocious. As a general rule a lion is an amiable animal enough if he is left alone, but a hungry lion is almost as dangerous as a hungry man. One hears a great many different opinions expressed as to whether or no the lion is remarkable for his courage, but the result of my experience is that very much depends upon the state of his stomach. A hungry lion will not stick at a trifle, whereas a full one will flee at a very small rebuke.

"Well, we hunted all about, and nothing could we see, not even a duiker or a bush buck; and at last, thoroughly tired and out of temper, we started on our way back to camp, passing over the brow of a steepish hill to do so. Just as we climbed the crest of the ridge I came to a stand, for there, about six hundred yards to my left, his beautiful curved horns outlined against the soft blue of the sky, I saw a noble koodoo bull *(Strepsiceros kudu)*. Even at that distance, for as you know my eyes are very keen, I could distinctly see the white stripes on its side when the light fell upon it, and its large and pointed ears twitch as the flies worried it.

"So far so good; but how were we to get at it? It was ridiculous to risk a shot at that great distance, and yet both the ground and the wind lay very ill for stalking. It seemed to me that the only chance would be to make a detour of at least a mile or more, and come up on the other side of the koodoo. I called Harry to my side, and explained to him what I thought would be our best course, when suddenly, without any delay, the koodoo saved us further trouble by suddenly starting off down the hill like a leaping rocket. I do not know what had frightened it, certainly we had not. Perhaps a hyæna or a leopard—a tiger as we call it there—had suddenly appeared; at any rate, off it went, running slightly towards us, and I never saw a buck go faster. I am afraid that forgetting Harry's presence I used strong language, and really there was some excuse. As for Harry, he stood watching the beautiful animal's course. Presently it vanished behind a patch of bush, to emerge a few seconds later about five hundred paces from us, on a stretch of comparatively level ground that was strewn with boulders. On it went, clearing the boulders in its path with a succession of great bounds that were beautiful to behold. As it did so, I happened to look round at Harry, and perceived to my astonishment that he had got his rifle to his shoulder.

"'You young donkey!' I exclaimed, 'surely you are not going to'—and just at that moment the rifle went off.

"And then I think I saw what was in its way one of the most wonderful things I ever remember in my hunting experience. The koodoo was at the moment in the air, clearing a pile of stones with its fore-legs tucked up underneath it. All of an instant the legs stretched themselves out in a spasmodic fashion, it lit on them, and they doubled up beneath it. Down went the noble buck, down upon his head. For a moment he seemed to be standing on his horns, his hind-legs high in the air, and then over he rolled and lay still.

"'Great Heavens!' I said, 'why, you've hit him! He's dead.'

"As for Harry, he said nothing, but merely looked scared, as well he might, for such a marvellous, I may say such an appalling and ghastly fluke it has never been my lot to witness. A man, let alone a boy, might have fired a thousand such shots without ever touching the object; which, mind you, was springing and bounding over rocks quite five hundred yards away; and here this lad—taking a snap shot, and merely allowing for speed and elevation by instinct, for he did not put up his sights—had knocked the bull over as dead as a door-nail. Well, I made no further remark, as the occasion was too solemn for talking, but merely led the way to where the koodoo had fallen. There he lay, beautiful and quite still; and there, high up, about half-way down his neck, was a neat round hole. The bullet had severed the spinal marrow, passing through the vertebræ and away on the other side.

"It was already evening when, having cut as much of the best meat as we could carry from the bull, and tied a red handkerchief and some tufts of grass to his spiral horns, which, by the way, must have been nearly five feet in length, in the hope of keeping the jackals and aasvögels (vultures) from him, we finally got back to camp, to find Pharaoh, who was getting rather anxious at our absence, ready to greet us with the pleasing intelligence that another ox was sick. But even this dreadful bit of intelligence could not dash Harry's spirits; the fact of the matter being, incredible as it may appear, I do verily believe that in his heart of hearts he set down the death of the koodoo to the credit of his own skill. Now, though the lad was a pretty shot enough, this of course was ridiculous, and I told him so plainly.

"By the time that we had finished our supper of koodoo steaks (which would have been better if the koodoo had been a little younger), it was time to get ready for Jim-Jim's murderess. Accordingly we determined again to expose the unfortunate sick ox, that was now absolutely on its last legs, being indeed scarcely able to stand. All the afternoon Pharaoh told us it had been walking round and round in a circle as cattle in the last stage of redwater generally do. Now it had come to a standstill, and was swaying to and fro with its head hanging down. So we tied him up to the stump of the tree as on the previous night, knowing that if the lioness did not kill him he would be dead by morning. Indeed I was afraid that he would die at once, in which case he would be of but little use as a bait, for the lion is a sportsmanlike animal, and unless he is very hungry generally prefers to kill his own dinner, though when that is once killed he will come back to it again and again.

"Then we again went through our experience of the previous night, sitting there hour after hour, till at last Harry fell fast asleep, and, though I am accustomed to this sort of thing, even I could scarcely keep my eyes open. Indeed I was just dropping off, when suddenly Pharaoh gave me a push.

"*Listen!*' he whispered.

"I was awake in a second, and listening with all my ears. From the clump of bush to the right of the lightning-shattered stump to which the sick ox was tied came a faint crackling noise. Presently it was repeated. Something was moving there, faintly and quietly enough, but still moving perceptibly, for in the intense stillness of the night any sound seemed loud.

"I woke up Harry, who instantly said, 'Where is she? where is she?' and began to point his rifle about in a fashion that was more dangerous to us and the oxen than to any possible lioness.

"'Be quiet!' I whispered, savagely; and as I did so, with a low and hideous growl a flash of yellow light sped out of the clump of bush, past the ox, and into the corresponding clump upon the other side. The poor sick creature gave a sort of groan, staggered round and then began to tremble. I could see it do so clearly in the moonlight, which was now very bright, and I felt a brute for having exposed the unfortunate animal to such agony as he must undoubtedly be undergoing. The lioness, for it was she, passed so quickly that we could not even distinguish her movements, much less fire. Indeed at night it is absolutely useless to attempt to shoot unless the object is very close and standing perfectly still, and then the light is so deceptive and it is so difficult to see the foresight that the best shot will miss more often than he hits.

"'She will be back again presently,' I said; 'look out, but for Heaven's sake don't fire unless I tell you to.'

"Hardly were the words out of my mouth when back she came, and again passed the ox without striking him.

"'What on earth is she doing?' whispered Harry.

"'Playing with it as a cat does with a mouse, I suppose. She will kill it presently.'

"As I spoke, the lioness once more flashed out of the bush, and this time sprang right over the doomed and trembling ox. It was a beautiful sight to see her clear him in the bright moonlight, as though it were a trick which she had been taught.

"'I believe that she has escaped from a circus,' whispered Harry; 'it's jolly to see her jump.'

"I said nothing, but I thought to myself that if it was, Master Harry did not quite appreciate the performance, and small blame to him. At any rate, his teeth were chattering a little.

"Then came a longish pause, and I began to think that the lioness must have gone away, when suddenly she appeared again, and with one mighty bound landed right on to the ox, and struck it a frightful blow with her paw.

"Down it went, and lay on the ground kicking feebly. She

put down her wicked-looking head, and, with a fierce growl of contentment, buried her long white teeth in the throat of the dying animal. When she lifted her muzzle again it was all stained with blood. She stood facing us obliquely, licking her bloody chops and making a sort of purring noise.

"'Now's our time,' I whispered, 'fire when I do.'

"I got on to her as well as I could, but Harry, instead of waiting for me as I told him, fired before I did, and that of course hurried me. But when the smoke cleared, I was delighted to see that the lioness was rolling about on the ground behind the body of the ox, which covered her in such a fashion, however, that we could not shoot again to make an end of her.

"'She's done for! She's dead, the yellow devil!' yelled Pharaoh in exultation; and at that very moment the lioness, with a sort of convulsive rush, half-rolled, half-sprang, into the patch of thick bush to the right. I fired after her as she went, but so far as I could see without result; indeed the probability is that I missed her clean. At any rate she got to the bush in safety, and once there, began to make such a diabolical noise as I never heard before. She would whine and shriek with pain, and then burst out into perfect volleys of roaring that shook the whole place.

"'Well,' I said, 'we must just let her roar; to go into that bush after her at night would be madness.'

"At that moment, to my astonishment and alarm, there came an answering roar from the direction of the river, and then another from behind the swell of bush. Evidently there were more lions about. The wounded lioness redoubled her efforts, with the object, I suppose, of summoning the others to her assistance. At any rate they came, and quickly too, for within five minutes, peeping through the bushes of our skerm fence, we saw a magnificent lion bounding along towards us, through the tall tambouki grass, that in the moonlight looked for all the world like ripening corn. On he came in great leaps, and a glorious sight it was to see him. When within fifty yards or so, he stood still in an open space and roared. The lioness roared too; then there came a third roar, and another great black-maned lion stalked majestically up, and joined number two, till really I began to realize what the ox must have undergone.

"'Now, Harry,' I whispered, 'whatever you do don't fire, it's too risky. If they let us be, let them be.'

"Well, the pair marched off to the bush, where the wounded lioness was now roaring double tides, and the three of them began to snarl and grumble away together there. Presently, however, the lioness ceased roaring, and the two lions came out again, the black-maned one first— to prospect, I suppose— walked to where the carcass of the ox lay, and sniffed at it.

"'Oh, what a shot!' whispered Harry, who was trembling with excitement.

"'Yes,' I said; 'but don't fire; they might all of them come for us.'

"Harry said nothing, but whether it was from the natural impetuosity of youth, or because he was thrown off his balance by excitement, or from sheer recklessness and devilment, I am sure I cannot tell you, never having been able to get a satisfactory explanation from him; but at any rate the fact remains, he, without word or warning, entirely disregarding my exhortations, lifted up his Westley Richards and fired at the black-maned lion, and, what is more, hit it slightly on the flank.

"Next second there was a most awful roar from the injured lion. He glared around him and roared with pain, for he was badly stung; and then, before I could make up my mind what to do, the great black-maned brute, clearly ignorant of the cause of his hurt, sprang right at the throat of his companion, to whom he evidently attributed his misfortune. It was a curious sight to see the astonishment of the other lion at this most unprovoked assault. Over he rolled with an angry snarl, and on to him sprang the black-maned demon, and began to worry him. This finally awoke the yellow-maned lion to a sense of the situation, and I am bound to say that he rose to it in a most effective manner. Somehow or other he got to his feet, and, roaring and snarling frightfully, closed with his mighty foe.

"Then ensued a most tremendous scene. You know what a

shocking thing it is to see two large dogs fighting with abandonment. Well, a whole hundred of dogs could not have looked half
so terrible as those two great brutes as they rolled and roared
and rent in their horrid rage. They gripped each other, they tore
at each other's throat, till their manes came out in handfuls, and
the red blood streamed down their yellow hides. It was an awful
and a wonderful thing to see the great cats tearing at each other
with all the fierce energy of their savage strength, and making
the night hideous with their heart-shaking noise. And the fight
was a grand one too. For some minutes it was impossible to say
which was getting the best of it, but at last I saw that the black-
maned lion, though he was slightly bigger, was failing. I am inclined to think that the wound in his flank crippled him. Anyway,
he began to get the worst of it, which served him right, as he was
the aggressor. Still I could not help feeling sorry for him, for he
had fought a gallant fight, when his antagonist finally got him by
the throat, and, struggle and strike out as he would, began to
shake the life out of him. Over and over they rolled together, a
hideous and awe-inspiring spectacle, but the yellow one would
not loose his hold, and at length poor black-mane grew faint, his
breath came in great snorts and seemed to rattle in his nostrils,
then he opened his huge mouth, gave the ghost of a roar, quivered, and was dead.

"When he was quite sure that the victory was his own, the
yellow-maned lion loosed his grip and sniffed at the fallen foe.
Then he licked the dead lion's eye, and next, with his fore-feet
resting on the carcass, sent up his own chant of victory, that went
rolling and pealing down the dark paths of the night. And at this
point I interfered. Taking a careful sight at the centre of his body,
in order to give the largest possible margin for error, I fired, and
sent a .570 express bullet right through him, and down he
dropped dead upon the carcass of his mighty foe.

"After that, fairly satisfied with our performances, we slept
peaceably till dawn, leaving Pharaoh to keep watch in case any
more lions should take it into their heads to come our way.

"When the sun was well up we arose, and went very cautiously—at least Pharaoh and I did, for I would not allow Harry to come—to see if we could find any trace of the wounded lioness. She had ceased roaring immediately upon the arrival of the two lions, and had not made a sound since, from which we concluded that she was probably dead. I was armed with my express, while Pharaoh, in whose hands a rifle was indeed a dangerous weapon, to his companions, had an axe. On our way we stopped to look at the two dead lions. They were magnificent animals, both of them, but their pelts were entirely spoiled by the terrible mauling they had given to each other, which was a sad pity.

"In another minute we were following the blood spoor of the wounded lioness into the bush, where she had taken refuge. This, I need hardly say, we did with the utmost caution; indeed, I for one did not at all like the job, and was only consoled by the reflection that it was necessary, and that the bush was not thick. Well, we stood there, keeping as far from the trees as possible, searching and looking about, but no lioness could we see, though we saw plenty of blood.

"'She must have gone somewhere to die, Pharaoh,' I said in Zulu.

"'Yes, Inkoos,' he answered, 'she has certainly gone away.'

"Hardly were the words out of his mouth, when I heard a roar, and starting round saw the lioness emerge from the very centre of a bush, in which she had been curled up, just behind Pharaoh. Up she went on to her hind-legs, and as she did so I noticed that one of her fore-paws was broken near the shoulder, for it hung limply down. Up she went, towering right over Pharaoh's head, as she did so lifting her uninjured paw to strike him to the earth. And then, before I could get my rifle round or do anything to avert the oncoming catastrophe, the Zulu did a very brave and clever thing. Realizing his own imminent danger, he bounded to one side, and swinging the heavy axe round his head, brought it down right on to the back of the lioness, severing the vertebræ and killing her instantaneously. It was wonderful to see her collapse all in a heap like an empty sack.

"'My word, Pharaoh!' I said, 'that was well done, and none

too soon.'

"'Yes,' he answered, with a little laugh, 'it was a good stroke, Inkoos. Jim-Jim will sleep better now.'

"Then, calling Harry to us, we examined the lioness. She was old, if one might judge from her worn teeth, and not very large, but thickly made, and must have possessed extraordinary vitality to have lived so long, shot as she was; for, in addition to her broken shoulder, my express bullet had blown a great hole in her middle that one might have put a fist into.

"Well, that is the story of the death of poor Jim-Jim and how we avenged it. It is rather interesting in its way, because of the fight between the two lions, of which I never saw the like in all my experience, and I know something of lions and their manners."

*   *   *

"And how did you get back to Pilgrim's Rest?" I asked Hunter Quatermain when he had finished his yarn.

"Ah, we had a nice job with that," he answered. "The second sick ox died, and so did another, and we had to get on as best we could with three harnessed unicorn fashion, while we pushed behind. We did about four miles a day, and it took us nearly a month, during the last week of which we pretty well starved."

"I notice," I said, "that most of your trips ended in disaster of some sort or another, and yet you went on making them, which strikes one as a little strange."

"Yes, I dare say: but then, remember I got my living for many years out of hunting. Besides, half the charm of the thing lay in the dangers and disasters, though they were terrible enough at the time. Another thing is, my trips were not all disastrous. Some time, if you like, I will tell you a story of one which was very much the reverse, for I made several thousand pounds out of it, and saw one of the most extraordinary sights a hunter ever came across. It was on this trip that I met the bravest native woman I ever knew; her name was Maiwa. But it is too late now, and besides, I am tired of talking about myself. Pass the water, will you!"

THE MAHATMA AND THE HARE: A DREAM STORY

"Ultimately a good hare was found which took the field . . . There the hounds pressed her, and on the hunt arriving at the edge of the cliff the hare could be seen crossing the beach and going right out to sea. A boat was procured, and the master and some others rowed out to her just as she drowned, and, bringing the body in, gave it to the hounds. A hare swimming out to sea is a sight not often witnessed."

—Local paper, January 1911.

". . . A long check occurred in the latter part of this hunt, the hare having laid up in a hedgerow, from which she was at last evicted by a crack of the whip. Her next place of refuge was a horse-pond, which she tried to swim, but got stuck in the ice midway, and was sinking, when the huntsman went in after her. It was a novel sight to see huntsman and hare being lifted over a wall out of the pond, the eager pack waiting for their prey behind the wall."

—Local paper, February 1911.

The author supposes that the first of the above extracts must have impressed him. At any rate, on the night after the reading of it, just as he went to sleep, or on the following morning just as he awoke, he cannot tell which, there came to him the title and the outlines of this fantasy, including the command with which it ends. With a particular clearness did he seem to see the picture of the Great White Road, "straight as the way of the Spirit, and broad as the breast of Death," and of the little Hare travelling towards the awful Gates.

Like the Mahatma of this fable, he expresses no opinion as to the merits of the controversy between the Red-faced Man and the Hare that, without search on his own part, presented itself to his mind in so odd a fashion. It is one on which anybody interested in such matters can form an individual judgment.

THE MAHATMA[4]

Everyone has seen a hare, either crouched or running in the fields, or hanging dead in a poulterer's shop, or lastly pathetic, even dreadful-looking and in this form almost indistinguishable from a skinned cat, on the domestic table. But not many people have met a Mahatma, at least to their knowledge. Not many people know even who or what a Mahatma is. The majority of those who chance to have heard the title are apt to confuse it with another, that of Mad Hatter.

This is even done of malice prepense (especially, for obvious reasons, if a hare is in any way concerned) in scorn, not in ignorance, by persons who are well acquainted with the real meaning of the word and even with its Sanscrit origin. The truth is that an incredulous Western world puts no faith in Mahatmas. To it a Mahatma is a kind of spiritual Mrs. Harris, giving an address in Thibet at which no letters are delivered. Either, it says, there is no such person, or he is a fraudulent scamp with no greater occult powers—well, than a hare.

I confess that this view of Mahatmas is one that does not surprise me in the least. I never met, and I scarcely expect to meet, an individual entitled to set "Mahatma" after his name. Certainly *I* have no right to do so, who only took that title on the spur of the moment when the Hare asked me how I was called, and now make use of it as a *nom-de-plume*. It is true there is Jorsen, by whose order, for it amounts to that, I publish this history. For aught I know Jorsen may be a Mahatma, but he does not in the least look the part.

Imagine a bluff person with a strong, hard face, piercing grey eyes, and very prominent, bushy eyebrows, of about fifty or sixty years of age. Add a Scotch accent and a meerschaum pipe,

4 Mahatma, "great-souled." "One of a class of persons with preternatural powers, imagined to exist in India and Thibet." —*New English Dictionary*

which he smokes even when he is wearing a frock coat and a tall hat, and you have Jorsen. I believe that he lives somewhere in the country, is well off, and practises gardening. If so he has never asked me to his place, and I only meet him when he comes to Town, as I understand, to visit flower-shows.

Then I always meet him because he orders me to do so, not by letter or by word of mouth but in quite a different way. Suddenly I receive an impression in my mind that I am to go to a certain place at a certain hour, and that there I shall find Jorsen. I do go, sometimes to an hotel, sometimes to a lodging, sometimes to a railway station or to the corner of a particular street and there I do find Jorsen smoking his big meerschaum pipe. We shake hands and he explains why he has sent for me, after which we talk of various things. Never mind what they are, for that would be telling Jorsen's secrets as well as my own, which I must not do.

It may be asked how I came to know Jorsen. Well, in a strange way. Nearly thirty years ago a dreadful thing happened to me. I was married and, although still young, a person of some mark in literature. Indeed even now one or two of the books which I wrote are read and remembered, although it is supposed that their author has long left the world.

The thing which happened was that my wife and our daughter were coming over from the Channel Islands, where they had been on a visit (she was a Jersey woman), and, and—well, the ship was lost, that's all. The shock broke my heart, in such a way that it has never been mended again, but unfortunately did not kill me.

Afterwards I took to drink and sank, as drunkards do. Then the river began to draw me. I had a lodging in a poor street at Chelsea, and I could hear the river calling me at night, and—I wished to die as the others had died. At last I yielded, for the drink had rotted out all my moral sense. About one o'clock of a wild, winter morning I went to a bridge I knew where in those days policemen rarely came, and listened to that call of the water.

"Come!" it seemed to say. "This world is the real hell, ending in the eternal naught. The dreams of a life beyond and of re-union there are but a demon's mocking breathed into the mortal heart, lest by its universal suicide mankind should rob him of his torture-pit. There is no truth in all your father taught you" (he was a clergyman and rather eminent in his profession), "there is no hope for man, there is nothing he can win except the deep hap-piness of sleep. Come and sleep."

Such were the arguments of that voice of the river, the old, familiar arguments of desolation and despair. I leant over the parapet; in another moment I should have been gone, when I be-came aware that someone was standing near to me. I did not see the person because it was too dark. I did not hear him because of the raving of the wind. But I knew that he was there. So I waited until the moon shone out for a while between the edges of two ragged clouds, the shapes of which I can see to this hour. It showed me Jorsen, looking just as he does to-day, for he never seems to change—Jorsen, on whom, to my knowledge, I had not set eyes before.

"Even a year ago," he said, in his strong, rough voice, "you would not have allowed your mind to be convinced by such argu-ments as those which you have just heard in the Voice of the river. That is one of the worst sides of drink; it decays the reason as it does the body. You must have noticed it yourself."

I replied that I had, for I was surprised into acquiescence. Then I grew defiant and asked him what he knew of the argu-ments which were or were not influencing me. To my sur-prise—no, that is not the word—to my bewilderment, he repeated them to me one by one just as they had arisen a few minutes before in my heart. Moreover, he told me what I had been about to do, and why I was about to do it.

"You know me and my story," I muttered at last.

"No," he answered, "at least not more than I know that of many men with whom I chance to be in touch. That is, I have not met you for nearly eleven hundred years. A thousand and eighty-six, to be correct. I was a blind priest then and you were the captain of Irene's guard."

At this news I burst out laughing and the laugh did me good.

"I did not know I was so old," I said.

"Do you call that old?" answered Jorsen. "Why, the first time that we had anything to do with each other, so far as I can learn, that is, was over eight thousand years ago, in Egypt before the beginning of recorded history."

"I thought that I was mad, but you are madder," I said.

"Doubtless. Well, I am so mad that I managed to be here in time to save you from suicide, as once in the past you saved me, for thus things come round. But your rooms are near, are they not? Let us go there and talk. This place is cold and the river is always calling."

That was how I came to know Jorsen, whom I believe to be one of the greatest men alive. On this particular night that I have described he told me many things, and since then he has taught me much, me and a few others. But whether he is what is called a Mahatma I am sure I do not know. He has never claimed such a rank in my hearing, or indeed to be anything more than a man who has succeeded in winning a knowledge of his own powers out of the depths of the dark that lies behind us. Of course I mean out of his past in other incarnations long before he was Jorsen. Moreover, by degrees, as I grew fit to bear the light, he showed me something of my own, and of how the two were intertwined.

But all these things are secrets of which I have perhaps no right to speak at present. It is enough to say that Jorsen changed the current of my life on that night when he saved me from death.

For instance, from that day onwards to the present time I have never touched the drink which so nearly ruined me. Also the darkness has rolled away, and with it every doubt and fear; I know the truth, and for that truth I live. Considered from certain aspects such knowledge, I admit, is not altogether desirable. Thus it has deprived me of my interest in earthly things.

Ambition has left me altogether; for years I have had no wish to succeed in the profession which I adopted in my youth, or in any other. Indeed I doubt whether the elements of worldly success still remain in me; whether they are not entirely burnt away by that fire of wisdom in which I have bathed. How can we strive to win a crown we have no longer any desire to wear? Now I desire other crowns and at times I wear them, if only for a little while. My spirit grows and grows. It is dragging at its strings.

What am I to look at? A small, white-haired man with a thin and rather plaintive face in which are set two large, dark eyes that continually seem to soften and develop. That is my picture. And what am I in the world? I will tell you. On certain days of the week I employ myself in editing a trade journal that has to do with haberdashery. On another day I act as auctioneer to a firm which imports and sells cheap Italian statuary; modern, very modern copies of the antique, florid marble vases, and so forth. Some of you who read may have passed such marts in different parts of the city, or even have dropped in and purchased a bust or a tazza for a surprisingly small sum. Perhaps I knocked it down to you, only too pleased to find a *bona fide* bidder amongst my company.

As for the rest of my time—well, I employ it in doing what good I can among the poor and those who need comfort or who are bereaved, especially among those who are bereaved, for to such I am sometimes able to bring the breath of hope that blows from another shore.

Occasionally also I amuse myself in my own fashion. Thus sure knowledge has come to me about certain epochs in the past in which I lived in other shapes, and I study those epochs, hoping that one day I may find time to write of them and of the parts I played in them. Some of these parts are extremely interesting, especially as I am of course able to contrast them with our modern modes of thought and action.

They do not all come back to me with equal clearness, the earlier lives being, as one might expect, the more difficult to recover and the comparatively recent ones the easiest. Also they seem to range over a vast stretch of time, back indeed to the days of primeval, prehistoric man. In short, I think the subconscious in some ways resembles the conscious and natural memory; that which is very far off to it grows dim and blurred, that which is comparatively close remains clear and sharp, although of course this rule is not invariable. Moreover there is foresight as well as memory. At least from time to time I seem to come in touch with future events and states of society in which I shall have my share.

I believe some thinkers hold a theory that such conditions as those of past, present, and future do not in fact exist; that everything already is, standing like a completed column between earth and heaven; that the sum is added up, the equation worked out. At times I am tempted to believe in the truth of this proposition. But if it be true, of course it remains difficult to obtain a clear view of other parts of the column than that in which we happen to find ourselves objectively conscious at any given period, and needless to say impossible to see it from base to capital.

However this may be, no individual entity pervades all the column. There are great sections of it with which that entity has nothing to do, although it always seems to appear again above. I suppose that those sections which are empty of an individual and his atmosphere represent the intervals between his lives which he spends in sleep, or in states of existence with which this world is not concerned, but of such gulfs of oblivion and states of being I know nothing.

To take a single instance of what I do know: once this spirit of mine, that now by the workings of destiny for a little while occupies the body of a fourth-rate auctioneer, and of the editor of a trade journal, dwelt in that of a Pharaoh of Egypt—never mind which Pharoah. Yes, although you may laugh and think me mad to say it, for me the legions fought and thundered; to me the peoples bowed and the secret sanctuaries were opened that I and I alone might commune with the gods; I who in the flesh and after it myself was worshipped as a god.

Well, of this forgotten Royalty of whom little is known save what a few inscriptions have to tell, there remains a portrait statue in the British Museum. Sometimes I go to look at that statue and try to recall exactly under what circumstances I caused it to be shaped, puzzling out the story bit by bit.

Not long ago I stood thus absorbed and did not notice that the hour of the closing of the great gallery had come. Still I stood and gazed and dreamt till the policeman on duty, seeing and suspecting me, came up and roughly ordered me to begone.

The man's tone angered me. I laid my hand on the foot of the statue, for it had just come back to me that it was a "Ka" image, a sacred thing, any Egyptologist will know what I mean, which for ages had sat in a chamber of my tomb. Then the Ka that clings to it eternally awoke at my touch and knew me, or so I suppose. At least I felt myself change. A new strength came into me; my shape, battered in this world's storms, put on something of its ancient dignity; my eyes grew royal. I looked at that man as Pharaoh may have looked at one who had done him insult. He saw the change and trembled—yes, trembled. I believe he thought I was some imperial ghost that the shadows of evening had caused him to mistake for man; at any rate he gasped out—

"I beg your pardon, I was obeying orders. I hope your Majesty won't hurt me. Now I think of it I have been told that things come out of these old statues in the night."

Then turning he ran, literally ran, where to I am sure I do not know, probably to seek the fellowship of some other policeman. In due course I followed, and, lifting the bar at the end of the hall, departed without further question asked. Afterwards I was very glad to think that I had done the man no injury. At the moment I knew that I could hurt him if I would, and what is more I had the desire to do so. It came to me, I suppose, with that breath of the past when I was so great and absolute. Perhaps I, or that part of me then incarnate, was a tyrant in those days, and this is why now I must be so humble. Fate is turning my pride to its hammer and beating it out of me.

For thus in the long history of the soul it serves all our vices.

THE GREAT WHITE ROAD

Now, as I have hinted, under the teaching of Jorsen, who saved me from degradation and self-murder, yes, and helped me with money until once again I could earn a livelihood, I have acquired certain knowledge and wisdom of a sort that are not common. That is, Jorsen taught me the elements of these things; he set my feet upon the path which thenceforward, having the sight, I have been able to follow for myself. How I followed it does not matter, nor could I teach others if I would.

I am no member of any mystic brotherhood, and, as I have explained, no Mahatma, although I have called myself thus for present purposes because the name is a convenient cloak. I repeat that I am ignorant if there are such people as Mahatmas, though if so I think Jorsen must be one of them. Still he never told me this. What he has told is that every individual spirit must work out its own destiny quite independently of others. Indeed, being rather fond of fine phrases, he has sometimes spoken to me of, or rather, insisted upon what he called "the lonesome splendour of the human soul," which it is our business to perfect through various lives till I can scarcely appreciate and am certainly unable to describe.

To tell the truth, the thought of this "lonesome splendour" to which it seems some of us may attain, alarms me. I have had enough of being lonesome, and I do not ask for any particular splendour. My only ambitions are to find those whom I have lost, and in whatever life I live to be of use to others. However, as I gather that the exalted condition to which Jorsen alludes is thousands of ages off for any of us, and may after all mean something quite different to what it seems to mean, the thought of it does not trouble me over much. Meanwhile what I seek is the vision of those I love.

Now I have this power. Occasionally when I am in deep sleep some part of me seems to leave my body and to be transported quite outside the world. It travels, as though I were already dead, to the Gates that all who live must pass, and there takes its stand, on the Great White Road, watching those who have been called speed by continually. Those upon the earth know nothing of that Road. Blinded by their pomps and vanities, they cannot see, they will not see it always growing towards the feet of every one of them. But I see and know. Of course you who read will say that this is but a dream of mine, and it may be. Still, if so, it is a very wonderful dream, and except for the change of the passing people, or rather of those who have been people, always very much the same.

There, straight as the way of the Spirit and broad as the breast of Death, is the Great White Road running I know not whence, up to those Gates that gleam like moonlight and are higher than the Alps. There beyond the Gates the radiant Presences move mysteriously. Thence at the appointed time the Voice cries and they are opened with a sound like to that of deepest thunder, or sometimes are burned away, while from the Glory that lies beyond flow the sweet-faced welcomers to greet those for whom they wait, bearing the cups from which they give to drink. I do not know what is in the cups, whether it be a draught of Lethe or some baptismal water of new birth, or both; but always the thirsting, world-worn soul appears to change, and then as it were to be lost in the Presence that gave the cup. At least they are lost to my sight. I see them no more.

Why do I watch those Gates, in truth or in dream, before my time? Oh! You can guess. That perchance I may behold those for whom my heart burns with a quenchless, eating fire. And once I beheld—not the mother but the child, my child, changed indeed, mysterious, wonderful, gleaming like a star, with eyes so deep that in their depths my humanity seemed to swoon.

She came forward; she knew me; she smiled and laid her finger on her lips. She shook her hair about her and in it vanished as in a cloud. Yet as she vanished a voice spoke in my heart, her voice, and the words it said were—

"Wait, our Beloved! Wait!"

Mark well. "Our Beloved," not "My Beloved." So there are others by whom I am beloved, or at least one other, and I know well who that one must be.

*　　　*　　　*

After this dream, perhaps I had better call it a dream, I was ill for a long while, for the joy and the glory of it overpowered me and brought me near to the death I had always sought. But I recovered, for my hour is not yet. Moreover, for a long while as we reckon time, some years indeed, I obeyed the injunction and sought the Great White Road no more. At length the longing grew too strong for me and I returned thither, but never again did the vision come. Its word was spoken, its mission was fulfilled. Yet from time to time I, a mortal, seem to stand upon the borders of that immortal Road and watch the newly dead who travel it towards the glorious Gates.

Once or twice there have been among them people whom I have known. As these pass me I appear to have the power of looking into their hearts, and there I read strange things. Sometimes they are beautiful things and sometimes ugly things. Thus I have learned that those I thought bad were really good in the main, for who can claim to be quite good? And on the other hand that those I believed to be as honest as the day —well, had their faults.

To take an example which I quote because it is so absurd. The rooms I live in were owned by a prim old woman who for more than twenty years was my landlady. She and I were great friends, indeed she tended me like a mother, and when I was so ill nursed me as perhaps few mothers would have done. Yet while I was watching on the Road suddenly she came by, and with horror I saw that during all those years she had been robbing me, taking, I am sorry to say, many things, in money, trinkets, and food. Often I had discussed with her where these articles could possibly have gone, till finally suspicion settled upon the man who cleaned the windows. Yes, and worst of all, he was prosecuted, and I gave evidence against him, or rather strengthened her evidence, on faith of which the magistrate sent him to prison for a month.

"Oh! Mrs Smithers," I said to her, "how *could* you do it, Mrs. Smithers?"

She stopped and looked about her terrified, so that my heart smote me and I added in haste, "Don't be frightened, Mrs. Smithers; I forgive you."

"I can't see you, sir," she exclaimed, or so I dreamed, "but there! I always knew you would."

"Yes, Mrs. Smithers," I replied; "but how about the window-cleaner who went to jail and lost his situation?"

Then she passed on or was drawn away without making any answer.

Now comes the odd part of the story. When I woke up on the following morning in my rooms, it was to be informed by the frightened maid-of-all-work that Mrs. Smithers had been found dead in her bed. Moreover, a few days later I learned from a lawyer that she had made a will leaving me everything she possessed, including the lease of her house and nearly £1000, for she had been a saving old person during all her long life.

Well, I sought out that window-cleaner and compensated him handsomely, saying that I had found I was mistaken in the evidence I gave against him. The rest of the property I kept, and I hope that it was not wrong of me to do so. It will be remembered that some of it was already my own, temporarily diverted into another channel, and for the rest I have so many to help. To be frank I do not spend much upon myself.

THE HARE

Now I have done with myself, or rather with my own insignificant present history, and come to that of the Hare. It impressed me a good deal at the time, which is not long ago, so much indeed that I communicated the facts to Jorsen. He ordered me to publish them, and what Jorsen orders must be done. I don't know why this should be, but it is so. He has authority of a sort that I am unable to define.

One night after the usual aspirations and concentration of mind, which by the way are not always successful, I passed into what occultists call spirit, and others a state of dream. At any rate I found myself upon the borders of the Great White Road, as near to the mighty Gates as I am ever allowed to come. How far that may be away I cannot tell. Perhaps it is but a few yards and perhaps it is the width of this great world, for in that place which my spirit visits time and distance do not exist. There all things are new and strange, not to be reckoned by our measures. There the sight is not our sight nor the hearing our hearing. I repeat that all things are different, but that difference I cannot describe, and if I could it would prove past comprehension.

There I sat by the borders of the Great White Road, my eyes fixed upon the Gates above which the towers mount for miles on miles, outlined against an encircling gloom with the radiance of the world beyond the worlds. Four-square they stand, those towers, and fourfold the gates that open to the denizens of other earths. But of these I have no knowledge beyond the fact that it is so in my visions.

I sat upon the borders of the Road, my eyes fixed in hope upon the Gates, though well I knew that the hope would never be fulfilled, and watched the dead go by.

They were many that night. Some plague was working in the East and unchaining thousands. The folk that it loosed were strange to me who in this particular life have seldom left England, and I studied them with curiosity; high-featured, dark-hued people with a patient air. The knowledge which I have told me that one and all they were very ancient souls who often and often had walked this Road before, and therefore, although as yet they did not know it, were well accustomed to the journey. No, I am wrong, for here and there an individual did know. Indeed one deep-eyed, wistful little woman, who carried a baby in her arms, stopped for a moment and spoke to me.

"The others cannot see you as I do," she said. "Priest of the Queen of Queens, I know you well; hand in hand we climbed by the seven stairways to the altars of the moon."

"Who is the Queen of Queens?" I asked.

"Have you forgotten her of the hundred names whose veils

we lifted one by one; her whose breast was beauty and whose eyes were truth? In a day to come you will remember. Farewell till we walk this Road no more."

"Stay—when did we meet?"

"When our souls were young," she answered, and faded from my ken like a shadow from the sea.

After the Easterns came many others from all parts of the earth. Then suddenly appeared a company of about six hundred folk of every age and English in their looks. They were not so calm as are the majority of those who make this journey. When I read the papers a few days later I understood why. A great passenger ship had sunk suddenly in mid ocean and they were all cut off unprepared.

When, followed by a few stragglers, these had passed and gathered themselves in the red shadow beneath the gateway towers waiting for the summons, an unusual thing occurred. For a few moments the Road was left quite empty. After that last great stroke Death seemed to be resting on his laurels. When thus unpeopled it looked a very vast place like to a huge arched causeway, bordered on either side by blackness, but itself gleaming with a curious phosphorescence such as once or twice I have seen in the waters of a summer sea at night.

Presently in the very centre of this illuminated desolation, whilst it was as yet far away, something caught my eye, something so strange to the place, so utterly unfamiliar that I watched it earnestly, wondering what it might be. Nearer and nearer it came, with curious, uncertain hops; yes, a little brown object that hopped.

"Well," I said to myself, "if I were not where I am I should say that yonder thing was a hare. Only what would a hare be doing on the Great White Road? How could a hare tread the pathway of eternal souls? I must be mistaken."

So I reflected whilst still the thing hopped on, until I became certain that either I suffered from delusions, or that it was a hare; indeed a particularly fine hare, much such a one as a friend of my old landlady, Mrs. Smithers, had once sent her as a Christmas present from Norfolk, which hare I ate.

A few more hops brought it opposite to my post of observation. Here it halted as though it seemed to see me. At any rate it sat up in the alert fashion that hares have, its forepaws hanging absurdly in front of it, with one ear, on which there was a grey blotch, cocked and one dragging, and sniffed with its funny little nostrils. Then it began to talk to me. I do not mean that it really talked, but the thoughts which were in its mind were flashed on to my mind so that I understood perfectly, yes, and could answer them in the same fashion. It said, or thought, thus:

"You are real. You are a man who yet lives beneath the sun, though how you came here I do not know. I hate men, all hares do, for men are cruel to them. Still it is a comfort in this strange place to see something one has seen before and to be able to talk even to a man, which I could never do until the change came, the dreadful change—I mean because of the way of it," and it seemed to shiver. "May I ask you some questions?"

"Certainly," I said or rather thought back.

"You are sure that they won't make you angry so that you hurt me?"

"I can't hurt you, even if I wished to do so. You are not a hare any longer, if you ever were one, but only the shadow of a hare."

"Ah! I thought as much, and that's a good thing anyhow. Tell me, Man, have you ever been torn to pieces by dogs?"

"Good gracious! No."

"Or coursed, or hunted, or caught in a trap, or shot all over your back, or twisted up in nets and choked in snares? Or have you swum out to sea to die more easily, or seen your mate and mother and father killed?"

"No, no. Please stop, Hare; your questions are very unpleasant."

"Not half so unpleasant as the things are themselves, I can assure you, Man. I will tell you my story if you like; then you can judge for yourself. But first, if you will, do you tell me why I am here. Have you seen more hares about this place?"

"Never, nor any other animals. No, I am wrong, once I saw a dog."

The Hare looked about it anxiously.

"A dog. How horrible! What was it doing? Hunting? If there are no hares here what could it be hunting? A rabbit, or a pheasant with a broken wing, or perhaps a fox? I should not mind so much if it were a fox. I hate foxes; they catch young hares when they are asleep and eat them."

"None of these things. I was told that it belonged to a little girl who died. That broke its heart, so that it died also when they shut her up in a box. Therefore it was allowed to accompany her here because it had loved so much. Indeed I saw them together, both very happy, and together they went through those gates."

"If dogs love little girls why don't they love hares, at least as anything likes to be loved, for the dog didn't want to eat the little girl, did it? I see you can't answer me. Now would you like me to tell you my story? Something inside of me is saying that I am to do so if you will listen; also that there is plenty of time, for I am not wanted at present, and when I am I can run to those gates much quicker than you could."

"I should like it very much, Hare. Once a prophet heard an ass speak in order to warn him. But since then, except very, very rarely in dreams, no creature has talked to a man, so far as I know. Perhaps you wish to warn me about something, or others through me, as the ass warned Balaam."

"Who is Balaam? I never heard of Balaam. He wasn't the man who fetches dead pheasants in the donkey-cart, was he? If so, I've seen him make the ass talk—with a thick stick. No? Well, never mind, I daresay I should not understand about him if you told me. Now for my story."

Then the Hare sat itself down, planting its forepaws firmly in front of it, as these animals do when they are on the watch, looked up at me and began to pour the contents of its mind into mine.

*   *   *

I was born, it said, or rather told me by thought transference, in a field of growing corn near to a big wood. At least I suppose I was born there, though the first thing I remember is playing about in the wheat with two other little ones of my own size, a brother and a sister that were born with me. It was at night, for a great, round, shining thing which I now know was the moon, hung in the sky above us. We gambolled together and were very happy, till presently my mother came—I remember how big she looked—and cuffed me with her paw because I had led the others away from the place where she had told us to stop, and given her a great hunt to find us. That is the first thing I remember about my mother. Afterwards she seemed sorry because she had hurt me, and nursed us all three, letting me have the most milk. My mother always loved me the best of us, because I was such a fine leveret, with a pretty grey patch on my left ear. Just as I had finished drinking another hare came who was my father. He was very large, with a glossy coat and big shining eyes that always seemed to see everything, even when it was behind him.

He was frightened about something, and hustled my mother and us little ones out of the wheat-field into the big wood by which it is bordered. As we left the field I saw two tall creatures that afterwards I came to know were men. They were placing wire-netting round the field—you see I understand now what all these things were, although of course I did not at the time. The two ends of the wire netting had nearly come together. There was only a little gap left through which we could run. Another young hare, or it may have been a rabbit, had got entangled in it, and one of the men was beating it to death with a stick. I remember that the sound of its screams made me feel cold down the back, for I had never heard anything like that before, and this was the first that I had seen of pain and death.

The other man saw us slipping through and ran at us with his stick. My mother went first and escaped him. Then came my sister, then I, then my brother. My father was last of all. The man hit with his stick and it came down thud along side of me, just touching my fur. He hit again and broke the foreleg of my brother. Still we all managed to get through into the wood, except my father who was behind.

"There's the old buck!" cried one of the men (I understand what he said now, though at the time it meant nothing to me). "Knock him on the head!"

So leaving us alone they ran at him. But my father was much too quick for them. He rushed back into the corn and afterwards joined us in the wood, for he had seen wire before and knew how to escape it. Still he was terribly frightened and made us keep in the wood till the following evening, not even allowing my mother to go to her form in the rough pasture on its other side and lie up there.

Also we were in trouble because my brother's forepaw was broken. It gave him a great deal of pain, so that he could not rest or sleep. After a while, however, it mended up in a fashion, but he was never able to run as fast as we could, nor did he grow so big. In the end the mother fox killed him, as I shall tell.

My mother asked my father what the men with the sticks were doing— for, you know, many animals can talk to each other in their own way, even if they are of different kinds. He told her that they were protecting the wheat to prevent us from eating it, to which she answered angrily that hares must live somehow, especially when they had young ones to nurse. My father replied that men did not seem to think so, and perhaps they had young ones also. I see now that my father was a philosophic hare—

*   *   *

But are you tired of my story?

"Not at all," I answered; "go on, please. It is very interesting to hear things described from the animal's point of view, especially when that animal has grown wise and learned to understand."

"Ah," answered the Hare. "I see what you mean. And it is odd, but I do understand. All has become clear to me. I don't know what happened when I died, but there came a change, and I knew that I who was but a beast always have been and still am a necessary part of everything as much as you are, though more helpless and humble. Yes, I am as ancient and as far-reaching as yourself, but how I began and how I shall end is dark to me. Well, I will go on with my story.

*   *   *

It must have been a moon or so later, after my mother had given up nursing me, that I went to lie out by myself. There was a big house on the hillside overlooking the sea, and near to it were gardens surrounded by a wall. Also outside of this wall was another patch of garden where cabbages grew. I found a way to those cabbages and kept it secret, for I was greedy and wanted them all for myself. I used to creep in at night and eat them, also some flowers with spiky leaves that grew round them which had a very fine flavour. Then after the dawn came I went to a form which I had made under a furze bush on the slope that ran down to the sea, and slept there.

One day I was awakened by something white, hard, and round which rolled gently and stopped still quite close to me. It was not alive, although it had a queer smell, and I wondered why it moved at all. Presently I heard voices and there appeared a little man, and with him somebody who was not a man because it was differently dressed and spoke in a higher voice. I saw that they had sticks in their hands and thought of running away, then that it would be safer to lie quite close. They came up to me and the little man said—

"There's the ball; pick it up, Ella, the lie is too bad."

She, for now I know it was what is called a girl, stooped to obey and saw my back.

"Tom," she said in a whisper, "here's a young hare on its form."

"Get out of the light," he answered, "and I'll kill it," and he lifted the stick he held, which had a twisted iron end.

"No," she said, "catch it alive; I want a hare to be a friend to my rabbit, which has lost all its little ones."

"Lost them? Eaten them, you mean, because you would always go and stare at it," said Tom. "Where's the leveret? Oh! I see. Now, look out!"

A moment later and I was in darkness. Tom had thrown himself upon the top of me and was grabbing at me with his hands. I nearly got away, but as my head poked up under his arm the girl caught hold of it.

"Oh! It's scratching," she cried, as indeed I was with all my might. "Hold it, Tom, hold it!"

"Hold it yourself," said Tom, "my face is full of furze prickles." So she held and presently he helped her, till in the end I was tied up in a pocket-handkerchief and carried I knew not whither. Indeed I was almost mad with fear.

When I came to myself I found that I was within a kind of wire run which smelt foully, as though hundreds of things had lived in it for years. There was a hutch at the end of the run in which sat an enormous she-rabbit, quite as big as my mother, a fierce-looking brute with long yellow teeth. I was afraid of that rabbit and got as far from it as I could. Presently it hopped out and looked at me.

"What are you doing here?" it asked. "Can't you talk? Well, it doesn't matter. If I get hungry I'll eat you! Do you hear that? I'll eat you, as I did all the others," and it showed its big yellow teeth and hopped back into the hutch.

After that Tom and the girl came and gave us plenty of food which the big rabbit ate, for I could touch nothing. For two days they came, and then I think they forgot all about us. I grew very hungry, and at night filled myself with some of the remaining food, such as stale cabbage leaves. By next morning all was gone, and the big rabbit grew hungry also. All that day it hopped about sniffing at me and showing its yellow teeth.

"I shall eat you to-night," it said.

I ran round and round the pen in terror, till at last I found a place where rats had been working under the wire, almost big enough for me to squeeze through, but not quite.

The sun went down and the big she-rabbit came out.

"Now I am going to eat you," it said, "as I ate all the others. I am hungry, very hungry," and it prodded me about with its nose and rolled me over.

At last with a little squeal it drove its big yellow teeth into me behind. Oh! How they hurt! I was near the rat-hole. I rushed at it, scrabbling and wriggling. The big rabbit pounced on me with its fore-feet, trying to hold me, but too late, for I was through, leaving some of my fur behind me. I ran, how I ran! Without stopping, till at length I found my mother in the rough pasture by the wood and told her everything.

"Ah!" she said, "that's what comes of greediness and of trying to be too clever. Now, perhaps, you will learn to stop at home."

So I did for a long while.

*   *   *

The summer went by without anything particular happening, except that my brother with the lame foot was eaten by the mother fox. That great red beast was always prowling about, and at night surprised us in a field near the wood where we were feeding on some beautiful turnips. The rest of us got away, but my brother being lame, was not quick enough. The fox caught him, and I heard her sharp white teeth crunch into his bones. The sound made me quite sick, and my mother was very sad afterwards. She complained to my father of the cruelty of foxes, but he, who, as I have said, was a philosopher, answered her almost in her own words.

"Foxes must live, and this one has young to feed, and therefore is always hungry. There are three of them in a hole at the top of the wood," he remarked. "Also our son was lame and would certainly have been caught when the hunting begins."

"What's the hunting?" I asked.

"Never mind," said my father sharply. "No doubt you'll find out in time, that is if you live through the shooting."

"What's the shooting?" I began, but my father cuffed me over the head and I was silent.

I may tell you that my mother soon got over the loss of my brother, for just about that time she had four new little ones, after which neither she nor my father seemed to think any more about us. My sister and I hated those little ones. We two alone remembered my brother, and sometimes wondered whether he was quite gone or would one day come back. The fox, I am glad to say, got caught in a trap. At least I am not glad now—I was glad because, you see, I was so much afraid of her.

THE SHOOTING

I was quite close by one morning when the fox, who was smelling about after me, I suppose because it had liked my brother so much, got caught in the big trap which was covered over artfully with earth and baited with some stuff which stank horribly. I remember it looked very like my own hind-legs. The fox, not being able to find me, went to this filth and tried to eat it.

Then suddenly there was a dreadful fuss. The fox yelped and flew into the air. I saw that a great black thing was fast on its forepaw. How that fox did jump and roll! It was quite wonderful to see her. She looked like a great yellow ball, except for a lot of white marks about the head, which were her teeth. But the trap would not come away, because it was tied to a root with a chain.

At last the fox grew tired and, lying down, began to think, licking its paw as it thought and making a kind of moaning noise. Next it commenced gnawing at the root after trying the chain and finding that its teeth would not go into it. While it was doing this I heard the sound of a man somewhere in the wood. So did the fox, and oh! It looked so frightened. It lay down panting, its tongue hanging out and its ears pressed back against its head, and whisked its big tail from side to side. Then it began to gnaw again, but this time at its own leg. It wanted to bite it off and so get away. I thought this very brave of the fox, and though I hated it because it had eaten my brother and tried to eat me, I felt quite sorry.

It was about half through its leg when the man came. I remember that he had a cat with a little red collar on its neck, and an owl in his hand, both of them dead, for he was Giles, the head-keeper, going round his traps. He was a tall man with sandy whiskers and a rough voice, and he carried a single-barrelled gun under his arm.

You see, now that I am dead I know the use of these things, just as I understand all that was said, though of course at the time it had no meaning for me. Still I find that I have forgotten nothing, not one word from the beginning of my life to the end.

The keeper, who was on his way to the place where he nailed the creatures he did not like by dozens upon poles, looked down and saw the fox. "Oh! My beauty," he said, "so I have got you at last.

Don't you think yourself clever trying to bite off that leg. You'd have done it too, only I came along just in time. Well, good night, old girl, you won't have no more of my pheasants."

Then he lifted the gun. There was a most dreadful noise and the fox rolled over and lay still.

"There you are, all neat and tidy, my dear," said the keeper. "Now I must just tuck you away in the hollow tree before old Grampus sneaks round and sees you, for if he should it will be almost as much as my place is worth."

Next he set his foot on the trap and, opening it, took hold of the fox by the fore-legs to carry it off. The cat and the owl he stuffed away into a great pocket in his coat.

"Jemima! Don't you wholly stink," he said, then gave a most awful yell.

The fox wasn't quite dead after all, it was only shamming dead. At any rate it got Giles' hand in its mouth and made its teeth meet through the flesh.

Now the keeper began to jump about just as the fox had done when it set its paw in the trap, shouting and saying all sorts of things that somehow I don't think I ought to repeat here. Round and round he went with the fox hanging to his hand, like hares do when they dance together, for he couldn't get it off anyhow. At last he tumbled down into a pool of mud and water, and when he got up again all wet through I saw that the fox was really dead. But it had died biting, and now I know that this pleased it very much.

It was just then that the man whom the keeper had called Grampus came up. He was a big, fat man with a very red face, who made a kind of blowing noise when he walked fast. I know now that he was the lord of all the other men about that place, that he lived in the house which looked over the sea, and that the boy and girl who put me in with the yellow-toothed rabbit were his children. He was what the farmers called "a first-rate all-round sportsman," which means—

*   *   *

"My friend—but what is your name?"

"Oh! Mahatma," I answered at hazard.

"Which means, my friend Mahatma, that he spent most of the year in killing the lower animals such as me. Yes, he spent quite eight months out of the twelve in killing us one way and another, for when there was no more killing to be done in his own country, he would travel to others and kill there. He would even kill pigeons from a trap, or young rooks just out of their nests, or rats in a stack, or sparrows among ivy, rather than not kill anything. I've heard Giles say so to the under-keeper and call him 'a regular slaughterer' and 'a true-blood Englishman.' Yet, my friend Mahatma, I say in the light of the truth which has come to me, that according to his knowledge Grampus was a good man. Thus, what little time he had to spare from sport he passed in helping his brother men by sending them to prison. Although of course he never worked or earned anything, he was very rich, because money flowed to him from other people who had been very rich, but who at last were forced to travel this Road and could not bring it with them. If they could have brought it, I am sure that Grampus would never have got any. However, he did get it, and he aided a great many people with that part of it which he found he could not spend upon himself. He was a very good man, only he liked killing us lower creatures, whom he bred up with his money to be killed."

"Go on with your story, Hare," I said; "when I see this Red-faced Man I will judge of him for myself. Probably you are prejudiced about him."

"I daresay I am," answered the Hare, rubbing its nose; "but please observe that I am not speaking unkindly of Grampus, although before I have done you may think that I might have reason to do so. However, you will be able to form your own opinion when he comes here, which I am sure he does not mean to do for many, many years. The world is much too comfortable for him. He does not wish to leave it."

"Still he may be obliged to do so, Hare."

"Oh! No, people like that are never obliged to do anything they do not like. It is only poor things such as you and I, Mahatma, which must suffer. I can see that you have had a great deal to bear, and so have I, for we were born to suffering as the Red-faced Man was born to happiness."

"Go on with your story, Hare," I repeated. "You are becoming metaphysical and therefore dull. The time is short and I want to hear what happened."

"Quite so, Mahatma."

*   *   *

Well, Grampus came up breathing very heavily and looking very red in the face. He held his hat in one hand and a large crooked stick in the other, and even the top of his head, on which no hair grew, was red, for he had been running.

"What the deuce is the matter?" he puffed. "Oh! It is you, Giles, is it? What are you doing, sir, looking like that, all covered with blood and mud? Has a poacher shot you, or what?"

"No, Squire," answered Giles humbly, touching his hat. "I have shot a poacher, that's all, and it has given me what for," and he lifted the body of the fox from the water.

"A fox," said Grampus, "a fox! Do you mean to say, Giles, that you have dared to shoot a fox, and a vixen with a litter too? How often have I told you that, although I keep harriers and not foxhounds, you are never to touch a fox. You will get me into trouble with all my neighbours. I give you a month's notice. You will leave on this day month."

"Very well, Squire," said Giles, "I'll leave, and I hope you'll find someone to serve you better. Meanwhile I didn't shoot the dratted fox. At least I only shot her after she'd gone and got herself into a trap which I had set for that there Rectory dog what you told me to make off with on the quiet, so that the young lady might never know what become of it and cry and make a fuss as she did about the last. Then seeing that she was finished, with her leg half chewed off, I shot her, or rather I didn't shoot her as well as I should, for the beggar gave a twist as I fired, and now she's bit me right through the hand. I only hopes you won't have to pay my widow for it, Squire, under the Act, as foxes' bites is uncommon poisonous, especially when they've been a-eating of rotten rabbit."

"Dear me!" said the Red-faced Man softening, "dear me, the beast does seem to have bitten you very badly. You must go and be cauterised with a red-hot iron. It is painful but the best thing to do. Meanwhile, suck it, Giles, suck it! I daresay that will draw out the poison, and if it doesn't, thank my stars! I am insured. Look here, a minute or two can make no difference, for if you are poisoned, you are poisoned. Where can we put this brute? I wouldn't have it seen for ten pounds."

"There's an old pollard, Squire, about five yards away down near the fence, which is hollow and handy," said Giles.

"Quite so," he answered, "I know it well. Do you bring the—dog, Giles. Remember, it was a dog, not a fox."

Then they went to the pollard, and as Giles's hand was hurt the Red-faced Man climbed up it, though Giles tried to prevent him.

"Now then, Giles," he said, "give me the fox—I mean the dog, and I will drop it down. Great Heavens! How this tree stinks. Has there been an earth here?"

"Not as I knows of, Squire," said Giles sullenly.

Grampus stretched his hand down into the hollow of the pollard and dragged up a rotting fox by its tail.

"Giles," he said, "you have been killing more foxes and hiding them in this tree. Giles, I dismiss you at once and without a month's wages."

"All right, sir," said Giles, "I'll go, and I prays you'll find some-one what will keep your hares which you must have, and your pheasants which you must have, and your partridges which you must have, without killing these varmints of foxes what eats the lot."

The Red-faced Man descended from the tree holding his nose and looked at Giles. Giles sucked his bleeding hand and looked at him.

"Foxes are very destructive animals," said the Red-faced Man to Giles, "especially when one shoots and keeps harriers."

"They are that, sir," said Giles to the Red-faced Man, "as only those know what has to do with them."

"Put the other in, Giles," said the Red-faced man, "and when you have time, throw some soil on to the top of the lot. This place smells horrible. And look you here, Giles," he added in a voice of thunder, "if ever I find you killing a fox upon this property, you will be dismissed at once, as I have often told you before. Do you understand?"

"Yes, Squire, I understand," answered Giles, "and I'll see to the burying of them this same afternoon, if the pain in my hand will suffer it."

"Very well," said the Red-faced Man, "that's done with—except the cubs. As you have killed the vixen you had better stink the cubs out of the earth. I daresay they are old enough to look after themselves— at any rate I hope so. And now, Giles, we must shoot some of these hares when we begin on the partridges next week. There are too many of them, the tenants are complaining, ungrateful beggars as they are, seeing that I keep them for their sport."

At this point I thought that I had heard enough, and slipped away when their backs were turned. For I had just seen a fox shot, and now I knew what shooting meant.

*　　*　　*

About a week later I knew better still. It came about thus. By that time the turnips I have mentioned, those that grew in the big field, had swelled into fine, large bulbs with leafy tops. We used to eat them at nights, and in the daytime to lie up among them in our snug forms. You know, Mahatma, don't you, that a form is a little hollow which a hare makes in the ground just to fit itself? No hare likes to sleep in another hare's form. Do you understand?"

"Yes," I answered, "I understand. It would be like a man wearing another man's boots."

"I don't know anything about boots, Mahatma, except that they are hard things with iron on them which kick one out of one's form if one sits too close. Once that happened to me. Well, my form was under a particularly fine turnip that had some dead leaves beneath the green ones. I chose it because, like the brown earth, they just matched the colour of my back. I was sleeping there quite soundly when my sister came and woke me.

*   *   *

"There are men in the field," she said, her eyes nearly starting out of her head with fear, for she was always very timid.

"I'm off."

"Are you?" I answered. "Well, I think I shall stop here where I shan't be noticed. If we begin jumping over those turnips they will see us."

"We might run down the rows, keeping our ears close to our backs," she remarked.

"No," I said, "there are too many bare patches."

At this moment a gun went 'bang' some way off; and my sister, like a wise hare, scuttled away at full speed for the wood. But I only made myself smaller than usual and lay watching and listening.

There was a good deal to see and hear; for instance, a covey of partridges, troublesome birds that come scratching and fidgeting about when one wants to sleep, were running to and fro in a great state of concern.

"They are after us," said the old cock.

"I remember the same thing last year. Come on, do."

"How can I with all these young ones to look after?" answered the hen. "Why, if once they are scattered I shall never find them again."

"Just as you like, you know best," said the cock. "Goodbye," and away he flew, while his wife and the rest ran to a little distance, scattered and squatted.

Presently, looking back over my shoulders without turning my head, as a hare can, I saw a line of men walking towards me. There was the Red-faced Man whom Giles called Grampus behind his back and Squire to his face. There was Giles himself, with his hurt hand tied up, holding a kind of stick with a slit in it from which hung a lot of dead partridges whose necks were in the slit. One of them was not dead or had come to life again, for it flapped in the stick trying to fly away. He held these in the hand that was tied up, and in the other, oh, horror! Was a dead hare bleeding from its nose. It looked uncommonly like my mother, but whether it were or no I couldn't be quite sure. At least from that day neither my sister nor I ever saw her again.

*　　*　　*

I suppose you haven't met her coming up this big white Road, have you, Mahatma?

"No, no," I answered impatiently, "I have already told you that you are the first hare I have ever seen upon the Road. Please get on with your story, or the Lights will change and the Gates be opened before I hear its end."

Just when I saw her I was thinking of running away, but the sight terrified me so much that I could not stir. You see, Mahatma, I really loved my mother as much as a hare can love anything, which is a good deal.

*　　*　　*

Well, beyond Giles was, who do you think? That dreadful boy, Tom, with a gun in his hand too. Did I say that they all had guns, except Giles and some beater men, only that Tom's was single-barrelled? Then there were others whom I need not describe, stretching to left and right, and worst of all, perhaps, there was Giles's great black dog, a silly-looking beast which always seemed to have its mouth open and its tongue hanging out, and to be wagging a big tail like the fox's, only black and more ragged.

As I watched, up got the old hen partridge and one of her young ones and flew towards me. The Red-faced Man lifted his gun and fired, once, twice, and down came first the mother partridge and then the young one. I forgot to say that Tom fired too at the old partridge, which fell dead quite close to me, leaving a lot of feathers floating in the air. As it fell Tom screeched out—

"I killed that, father."

This made the Red-faced Man very angry.

"You young scoundrel," he said, "how often have I told you not to shoot at my birds under my nose? No sportsman shoots at another man's birds, and as for killing it, you were yards under the thing. If you do it again I will send you home."

"Sorry, father," said Tom, adding in a low voice with a snigger, "I did kill it after all. Dad thinks no one can hit a partridge except himself."

Just then up jumped my father near to Giles, and came leaping in front of the Red-faced Man about twenty yards away from him.

"Mark hare!" shouted Giles, and Grampus, who was still glowering at Tom and had not quite finished pushing the cartridges into his gun, shut it up in a hurry and fired first one barrel and then the other. But my father, who was very cunning, jumped into the air at the first shot and ducked at the second, so that he was missed; at least I suppose that is why he was missed.

Giles grinned and the Red-faced Man said, "Damn!"

*   *   *

"What does 'damn' mean, Mahatma? It was a very favourite word with the Red-faced Man, but even now I can't quite understand it."

"Nor can I," I answered. "Go on."

"Well, my poor father next ran in front of Tom, who shot too and hit him in the hind legs so that he rolled over and over in the turnips, kicking and screaming. Have you ever heard a hare scream, Mahatma?"

"Yes, yes, it makes a horrid noise like a baby."

*   *   *

"Wiped your eye that time, Dad," cried Tom in an exultant voice.

"I don't know about wiping my eye," answered his father, turning quite purple with rage, "but I wish you would be good enough, Thomas, not to shoot my hares behind, so that they make that beastly row which upsets me" (I think that the Red-faced Man was really kind at the bottom) "and spoils them for the market. If you can't hit a hare in front, miss it like a gentleman."

"As you do, Dad," said Tom, sniggering again. "All right, I'll try."

"Giles," roared Grampus, pretending not to hear, "send your dog and fetch that hare. I can't bear its screeching."

So that great black dog rushed forward and caught my poor father in its big mouth, although he tried to drag himself away on his front paws, and after that I shut my eyes.

Then a lot of partridges got up and there was any amount of

banging, though most of them were missed. This made the Red-faced Man angrier than ever. He took off his hat and waved it, bellowing—

"Call back that brute of a dog of yours, Giles. Call it back at once or I'll shoot it."

So Giles called, "Nigger. Come you 'ere, Nigger! Nigg, Nigg, Nigg!"

But Nigger rushed about putting up partridges all over the place while Grampus stamped and shouted and every one missed everything, till at last Tom sat down on the turnips and roared with laughter.

At length, after Giles had beaten Nigger till he broke a stick over him, making him howl terribly, order was restored, and the line having reformed, began to march down on me. I was so frightened by what had happened to my father, and I think my mother, that I didn't remember what he, I mean my dead father, had told me, always to run away when there is a chance, as poor hares can only protect themselves by flight.

So as I had lost the chance I thought that I would just sit tight, hoping that they would not see me. Nor indeed would they if it hadn't been for that horrible Tom.

During the confusion the mother partridge which the Red-faced Man had shot had been forgotten by everybody except Tom. Tom, you see, was certain that he had shot it himself, being a very obstinate boy, and was determined to retrieve it as his own.

Now that partridge had fallen within a yard of me, with its beak and claws pointing to the sky, and when the line had passed where we lay Tom lagged behind to look for it. He did not find it then, whether he ever found it afterwards I am sure I don't know. But he found me.

"By Jove! Here's a hare," he said, and made a grab at me just as he had done in the furze bush.

Well, I went. Tom shot when I wasn't more than four yards from him, and the whole charge passed like a bullet between my hind legs and struck the ground under my stomach, sending up such a shower of earth and stones that I was knocked right over.

"I've hit it!" yelled Tom, as he crammed another cartridge into his single-barrelled gun.

By the time that it was loaded I was quite thirty yards away and going like the wind. Tom lifted the gun.

"Don't shoot!" roared the Red-faced Man.

"Mind that there boy!" bellowed Giles.

I was running down between two rows of turnips and presently butted into a lad who was bending over, I suppose to pick up a partridge. At any rate his tail—

*   *   *

"Do you call it his tail, Mahatma?

"That will do," I answered.

"Well, his tail was towards me; it looked very round and shiny. The shot from Tom's gun hit it everywhere. I wish they had all gone into it, but as he was so far away the charge scattered and six of the bullets struck me. Oh! They did hurt. Put your hand on my back, Mahatma, and you will feel the six lumps they made beneath the grey tufts of hair that grew over them, for they are still there."

Forgetting that we were on the Road, I stretched out my hand; but, of course, it went quite through the hare, although I could see the six little grey tufts clearly enough.

"You are foolish, Hare; you don't remember that your body is not here but somewhere else."

"Quite true, Mahatma. If it were here I could not be talking to you, could I? As a matter of fact, I have no body now. It is—oh, never mind where. Still, you can see the grey tufts, can't you? Well, I only hope that those shot hurt that fat boy half as much as they did me. No, I don't mean that I hope it now, I used to hope it."

*   *   *

My goodness! Didn't he screech, much worse than my father when his legs were broken. And didn't everybody else roar and shout, and didn't I dance? Off I went right over the fat boy, who had tumbled down, up to the end of the field, then so bewildered was I with shock and the burning pain, back again quite close to them.

But now nobody shot at me because they all thought the boy was killed and were gathered round him looking very solemn. Only I saw that the Red-faced Man had Tom by the neck and was kicking him hard.

After that I saw no more, for I ran five miles before I stopped, and at last lay down in a little swamp near the seashore to which my mother had once taken me. My back was burning like fire, and I tried to cool it in the soft slush.

THE COURSING

Quite a moon went by before I recovered from Tom's shot. At first I thought that I was going to die, for, although luckily none of my bones were broken, the pain in my back was dreadful. When I tried to ease the agony by rubbing against roots it only became worse, for the fur fell off, leaving sores upon which flies settled. I could scarcely eat or sleep, and grew so thin that the bones nearly poked through my pelt. Indeed I wanted very much to die, but could not. On the contrary, by degrees I recovered, till at last I was quite strong again and like other hares, except for the six little grey tufts upon my back and one hole through my right ear.

Now all this while I had lived in the swamp near the sea, but when my strength returned I thought of my old home, to which something seemed to draw me. Also there were no turnips near the swamp, and as the winter came on I found very little to eat there. So one day, or rather one night, I travelled back home.

As it happened the first hare that I met near the big wood was my sister. She was very glad to see me, although she had forgotten how we came to part, and when I spoke of our father and mother these did not seem to interest her. Still from that time forward we lived together more or less till her end came.

One day—this was after we had made our home in the big wood, as hares often do in winter—there was a great disturbance. When we tried to go out to feed at daylight we found little fires burning everywhere, and near to them boys who beat themselves and shouted. So we went back into the wood, where the pheasants were running to and fro in a great state of mind.

Some hours later, when the sun was quite high, men began to march about and scores of shots were fired a long way off, also a wounded cock-pheasant fell near to us and fluttered away, making a queer noise in its throat. It looked very funny stumbling along on one leg with its beak gaping and two of the long feathers in its tail broken.

"I know what this is," I said to my sister. "Let's be gone before they shoot us. I've had enough of being shot."

So off we went, rushing past a boy by his fire, who yelled and threw a stick at us. But as it happened, on the borders of the property of the Red-faced Man there were poachers who knew that hares would come out of the wood on this day of the shooting and had made ready for us by setting wire nooses in the gaps of the hedges through which we ran. I got my foot into one of these but managed to shake it off. My sister was not so lucky, for her head went into another of them. She kicked and tore, but the more she struggled the tighter drew the noose.

I watched her for a little while until one of the poachers ran up with a stick.

Then I went away, as I could not bear to see her beaten to death, and that was the end of my sister. So now I was the only one left alive of our family, except perhaps some younger brothers whom I did not know, though I think it was one of these that afterwards I saw shot quite dead by Giles. He went over and over and lay as still as though he had never moved in all his life. Death seems a very wonderful thing, Mahatma, but I won't ask you what it is because I perceive that you can't answer.

After this nothing happened to me for a long while. Indeed I had the best time of my life and grew very strong and big, yes, the strongest and biggest hare of any that I ever saw, also the swiftest of foot. Twice I was chased by dogs; once by Giles's black beast, Nigger, and once by that of a shepherd. Finding that I could run right away from them without exerting myself at all, I grew to despise dogs. Ah! Little did I know then that there are many different breeds of these animals.

One day in mid-winter, as the weather was very mild and open, I was lying on the rough grass field that I have spoken of which borders a flat stretch of moorland. On this moorland in summer grew tall ferns, but now these had died and been broken down by the wind. Suddenly I woke up from my sleep to see a number of men walking and riding towards me.

They were tenants and others who, although the real coursing season had not yet begun in our neighbourhood, had been asked by Grampus to come to try their greyhounds upon his land. Those of them who walked for the most part held two long, lean dogs on a string, while one or two carried dead hares. They were dreadful-looking hares that seemed to have been bitten all over; at least their coats were wet and broken. I shivered at the sight of them, feeling sure that I was going to be put to some new kind of torture.

Besides the men on foot were those on horseback, among whom I recognised the Red-faced Man and my enemy, the dreadful Tom. Most of the others were people called farmers, who seemed very happy and excited and from time to time drank something out of little bottles which they passed to each other. Giles was not there. Now I know that this was because he hated coursing, which killed down hares. Hares, he thought, out to be shot, not coursed.

Whilst I watched, wondering what to do, there was a shout of "There she goes!" and all the long dogs began to pull at their strings. Off the necks of two of them the collars seemed to fall, and away they leapt pursuing a hare. The men on the horses galloped after them, but the men on foot remained where they were.

Now I was afraid to get up and run lest they should loose the other dogs on me, so I lay still, till presently I saw the hare coming back towards me, followed by the two dogs whose noses almost touched its tail. It was exhausted and tried to twist and spring away to the right. But as it did so one of the dogs caught it in its mouth and bit it till it died.

"That was a rotten hare," said Tom, who cantered up just then, "it gave no course at all."

"Yes," puffed Grampus. "Hope the next one will show better sport."

"Hope so too," answered Tom, "especially as it is Jack and Jill's turn to be slipped, and they are the best greyhounds for twenty miles round."

Then the Red-faced Man gave some orders and Jack and Jill were brought forward by the man whose business it was to slip the dogs. One of them was black and one yellow; I think Jack was the black one—a dreadful, sneaking-looking beast with a white tip to its tail, which ended in a sort of curl.

"Forward now," said Grampus, "and go slow. There's sure to be another puss or two in this rough grass."

Next second I was up and away, and before you could count twelve Jack and Jill were after me. I saw them standing on their hind legs straining at the cord. Then the collars fell from them and they leapt forward like the light. My thought was to get back to the wood, which was about a minute's run behind me, but I did not dare to turn and head for it because of the long line of people through which I must pass if I tried to do so. So I ran straight for the moorland, hoping to turn there and reach the wood on its other side, although this meant a long journey.

For a while all went well with me, and having a good start I began to hope that I should outrun these beasts, as I had the shepherd's dog and the retriever. But I did not know Jack and Jill. Just as I reached the borders of the moor I heard the patter of their feet behind me, and looking back saw them coming up, about as far away as I was from Tom when he shot me.

They were running quite close together and behind them galloped the judge and other men. There was a fence here and I bolted through a hole in it. The greyhounds jumped over and for a moment lost sight of me, for I had turned and run down near the side of the fence. But Tom, who had come through a gap, saw me and waved his arm shouting, and next instant Jack and Jill saw me too.

Then as the going was rough by the fence I took to the open moor, always trying, however, to work round to the left in the hope that I might win the shelter of the wood.

On we went like the wind, and now Jack and Jill were quite close behind me, though before they got there I had managed to circle so that at last my head pointed to the wood, which was more than half a mile away. Their speed was greater than mine, and I knew that I must soon be caught.

At last they were not more than two yards behind, and for the first time I twisted so that they overshot me, which gave me another start. Three times they came up and three times I wrenched or twisted. The wood was not so far away now, but I was almost spent.

What was I to do! What was I to do! I saw a clump of furze to the left, a big clump and thick, and remembered that there was a hare's run through it. I reached it just as Jill was on the top of me, and once more they lost sight of me for a while as they ran round the clump staring and jumping. When they saw me again on the further side I was thirty yards ahead of them and the wood was perhaps two hundred and fifty yards away. But now I could only run more slowly, for my heart seemed to be bursting, though luckily Jack and Jill were getting tired also. Still they soon came up, and now I must twist every few yards, or be caught in their jaws.

I can't tell you what I felt, Mahatma, and until you have been hunted by greyhounds you will never know. It was horrible. Yet I managed to twist and jump so that always Jack and Jill just missed me. The farmers on the horses laughed to see my desperate leaps and wrenches.

But Tom did worse than laugh. Noting that I was getting quite near the wood, he rode between me and it, trying to turn me into the open, for he wished to see me killed.

"Don't do that! It isn't sportsmanlike," shouted the Red-faced Man. "Give the poor beast a chance."

I don't know whether he obeyed or not, as just then I made my last double, and felt Jill's teeth cut through the fur of my scut and heard them snap. I had dodged Jill, but Jack was right on to me and the wood still twenty yards away.

I could not twist any more, it was just which of us could get there first. I gathered all my remaining strength, for I was mad, mad with terror, and bounded forward.

After me came Jack, I felt his hot breath on my flank. I jumped the ditch, yes, I found power to jump that ditch where there was a rabbit run just by the trunk of a young oak. Jack jumped after me; we must both have been in the air at the same time. But I got through the rabbit run, whereas Jack hit his sharp nose against the trunk of the tree and broke his neck. Yes, he fell dead into the ditch.

I crawled on a few yards to a thick clump and squatted down, for I could not stir another inch. So it came about that I heard them all talking on the other side.

One of them said I was the finest hare he had ever coursed. Others, who had dragged Jack out of the ditch, lamented his death, especially the owner, who vowed that he was worth £50 and abused Tom. Tom, he said, had caused him to be killed—I don't know how, but I suppose because he had ridden forward and tried to turn me. The Red-faced Man also scolded Tom. Then he added—

"Well, I am glad she got off, for she'll give us a good run with the harriers one day. I shall always know that hare again by the white marks on its back; also it is the biggest I have seen for a long while. Come on, my friends, the dog is dead and there's an end of it. At least we have had a good morning's sport, so let's go to the Hall and get some lunch."

*   *   *

The Hare paused for a little, then looked up at me in its comical fashion and asked—

"Did you ever course hares, Mahatma?"

"Not I, thank goodness," I answered.

"Well, what do you think of coursing?"

"I would rather not say," I replied.

"Then I will," said the Hare, with conviction. "I think it horrible."

"Yes, but, Hare, you do not remember the pleasure this sport gives to the men and the dogs; you look at it from an entirely selfish point of view."

"And so would you, Mahatma, if you had felt Jack's hot breath on your back and Jill's teeth in your tail."

THE HUNTING

The Hare sat silent for a time, while I employed myself in watching certain shadows stream past us on the Great White Road. Among them was that of a politician whom I had much admired upon the earth. In this land of Truth I was grieved to observe certain characteristics about him which I had never before suspected. It seemed to me, alas! That in his mundane career he had not been so entirely influenced by a single-hearted desire for the welfare of our country as he had proclaimed and I had believed. I gathered even that his own interests had sometimes inspired his policy.

He went by, leaving, so far as I was concerned, a somewhat painful impression from which I sought relief in the company of the open-souled Hare.

"Well," I said, "I suppose that you died of exhaustion after your coursing experience, and came on here."

"Died of exhaustion, Mahatma, not a bit of it! In three days I was as well as ever, only much more cunning than I had been before. In the night I fed in the fields upon whatever I could get, but in the daytime I always lay up in woods. This I did because I found out the shooting was over, and I knew that greyhounds, which run by sight, would never come into woods."

*   *   *

The weeks went by and the days began to lengthen. Pretty yellow flowers that I had not seen before appeared in the woods, and I ate plenty of them; they have a nice flavour. Then I met another hare and loved her, because she reminded me of my sister. We used to play about together and were very happy. I wonder what she will do now that I am gone.

*   *   *

"Console herself with somebody else," I suggested sarcastically.

"No, she won't do that, Mahatma, because the hounds 'chopped' her just outside the Round Plantation. I mean they caught and ate her. You think that I am contradicting myself, but I am not. I mean I wonder what she will do without me in whatever world she has reached, for I don't see her here."

*   *   *

Well, I went to the little Round Plantation because I found that Giles seldom came there and I thought it would be safer, but as it proved I made a great mistake. One day there appeared the Red-faced Man and Tom and the girl, Ella, and a lot of other people mounted on horses, some of them dressed in green coats with ridiculous-looking caps on their heads.

Also with them were I don't know how many spotted dogs whose tails curled over their backs, not like greyhounds whose tails curl between their legs. Outside of the Plantation those dogs caught and ate my future wife, as I have said. It was her own fault, for I had warned her not to go there, but she was a very self-willed character. As it was she never even gave them a run, for they were all round her in a minute. Then they made a kind of cartwheel; their heads were in the centre of this cartwheel and their tails pointed out. In its exact middle was my future wife.

When the wheel broke up there was nothing of her left except her scut, which lay upon the ground.

I had seen so many of such things that I was not so much shocked as you might suppose. After all a fine hare like myself could always get another wife, and as I have told you she was very self-willed.

So I lay still, thinking that those men and dogs would go away.

But just as they were going the boy Tom called out—

"I say, Dad, I think we might as well knock through the Round Plantation. Giles tells me that the old speckle-backed buck lies up here."

"Does he?" said Grampus. "Well, if so, that's the hare I want to see, for I know he'd give us a good run. Here, Jerry" (Jerry was the huntsman), "just put the hounds into that place."

So Jerry put the hounds in, making dreadful noises to encourage them, and of course I came out, as I did not wish to share the fate of my future wife.

"That's him!" screeched Tom. "Look at the grey marks on his back."

"Yes, that's he right enough," shouted the Red-faced Man. "Lay them on, Jerry, lay them on; we're in for a rattling run now, I'll warrant."

So they were laid on and I went away as hard as my legs would carry me. Very soon I found that I had left all those curly-tailed dogs a long way behind.

"Ah!" I said to myself proudly, "these beasts are not grey-hounds; they are like Giles's retriever and the sheep dog. They'll never see me again. So I looped along saving my breath and head-ing for a wood which was quite five miles off that I had once vis-ited from the Marsh on the sea-shore where I lay sick, for I was sure they would never follow me there.

You can imagine, then, how surprised I was when I drew near that wood to hear a hideous noise of dogs all barking together be-hind me, and on looking back, to see those spotted brutes, with their tongues hanging out, coming along quite close to each other and not more than a quarter of a mile away.

Moreover they were coming after me. I was sure of that, for the first of them kept setting its nose to the ground just where I had run, and then lifting up its head to bay. Yes, they were coming on my scent. They could smell me as Giles's curly dog smells the wounded partridges. My heart sank at the thought, but presently I remembered that the wood was quite close, and that there I should certainly give them the slip.

So I went on quite cheerfully, not even running as fast as I could. But fortune was against me, as everything has always been, for I never found a friend. I ran along the side of a hedgerow which went quite up to the wood, not knowing that at the end of it three men were engaged in cutting down an oak tree. You see, they had caught sight of the hunt and stopped from their work, so that I did not hear the sound of their axes upon the tree. Nor, as my head was so near the ground, did I see them until I was right on to them, at which moment also they saw me.

"Here she is!" yelled one of them. "Keep her out of covert or they'll lose her," and he threw out his arms and began to jump about, as did the other two.

I pulled up short within three or four yards of them. Behind were the dogs and the people galloping upon horses and in front were the three men. What was I to do? Now I had stopped exactly in a gateway, for a lane ran alongside the wood. After a moment's pause I bolted through the gateway, thinking that I would get into the wood beyond. But one of the men, who of course wanted to see me killed, was too quick for me and there headed me again.

Then I lost my senses. Instead of running on past him and leaping into the wood, I swung right round and rushed back, still clinging to the hedgerow. Indeed as I went down one side of it the hounds and the hunters came up on the other, so that there were only a few sticks between us, though fortunately the wind was blowing from them to me. Fearing lest they should see me I jumped into the ditch and ran for quite two hundred yards through the mud and water that was gathered there. Then I had to come out of it again as it ended but here was a fall in the ground, so still I was not seen.

Meanwhile the hunt had reached the three men and I heard them all talking together. The end of it was that the men explained which way I had gone, and once more the hounds were laid on to me. In a minute they got to where I had entered the ditch, and there grew confused because my footmarks did not smell in the water. For quite a long time they looked about till at length, taking a wide cast, the hounds found my smell again at the end of the ditch.

During this check I was making the best of my way back towards my own home; indeed had it not been for it I should have been caught and torn to pieces much sooner than I was. Thus it happened that I had covered quite three miles before once more I heard those hounds baying behind me. This was just as I got on to the moorland, at that edge of it which is about another three miles from the great house called the Hall, which stands on the top of a cliff that slopes down to the beach and the sea.

I had thought of making for the other wood, that in which I had saved myself from the greyhounds when the beast Jack broke its neck against the tree, but it was too far off, and the ground was so open that I did not dare to try.

So I went straight on, heading towards the cliff. Another mile and they viewed me, for I heard Tom yell with delight as he stood up in his stirrups on the black cob he was riding and waved his cap. Jerry the huntsman also stood up in his stirrups and waved his cap, and the last awful hunt began.

I ran—oh! How I ran. Once when they were nearly on me I managed to check them for a minute in a hollow by getting among some sheep. But they soon found me again, and came after me at full tear not more than a hundred yards behind. In front of me I saw something that looked like walls and bounded towards them with my last strength. My heart was bursting, my eyes and mouth seemed to be full of blood, but the terror of being torn to pieces still gave me power to rush on almost as quickly as though I had just been put off my form. For as I have told you, I am, or rather was, a very strong and swift hare.

I reached the walls; there was an open doorway in them through which I fled, to find myself in a big garden. Two gardeners saw me and shouted loudly. I flew on through some other doors, through a yard, and into a passage where I met a woman carrying a pail, who shrieked and fell on to her back. I jumped over her and got into a big room, where was a long table covered with white on which were all sorts of things that I suppose men eat. Out of that room I went into yet another, where a fat woman with a hooked nose was seated holding something white in front of her. I bolted under the thing on which she was seated and lay there. She saw me come and began to shriek also, and presently a most terrible noise arose outside.

All the spotted dogs were in the house, baying and barking, and everybody was yelling. Then for a minute the dogs stopped their clamour, and I heard a great clatter of things breaking and of teeth crunching and of the Red-faced Man shouting—

"Those cursed brutes are eating the hunt lunch. Get them out, Jerry, you idiot! Get them out! Great heavens! What's the matter with her Ladyship? Is any one murdering her?"

I suppose that they couldn't get them out, or at least when they did they all came into the other room where I was under the seat on which the fat woman was now standing.

"What is it, mother?" I heard Tom say.

"An animal!" she screamed. "An animal under the sofa!"

"All right," he said, "that's only the hare. Here, hounds, out with her, hounds!"

The dogs rushed about, some of them with great lumps of food still in their mouths. But they were confused, and all went into the wrong places. Everything began to fall with dreadful crashes, the fat woman shrieked piercingly, and her shriek was—

"China! Oh! My china-a. John, you wretch! Help! Help! Help!"

To which the Red-faced Man roared in answer—

"Don't be an infernal fool, Eliza-a. I say, don't be such an infernal fool."

Also there were lots of other noises that I cannot remember, except one which a dog made.

This silly dog had thrust its head up the hole over a fire such as the stops make outside the coverts when men are going to shoot, either to hide something or to look for me there. When it came down again because the Red-faced Man kicked it, the dog put its paws into the fire and pulled it all out over the floor. Also it howled very beautifully. Just then another hound, that one which generally led the pack, began to sniff about near me and finally poked its nose under the stuff which hid me.

It jumped back and bayed, whereon I jumped out the other side. Tom made a rush at me and knocked the fat woman off the thing she was standing on, so that she fell among the dogs, which covered her up and began to sniff her all over. Flying from Tom I found myself in front of something filmy, beyond which I saw grass. It looked suspicious, but as nothing in the world could be so bad as Tom, no, not even his dogs, I jumped at it.

There was a crash and a sharp point cut my nose, but I was out upon the grass. Then there were twenty other crashes, and all the hounds were out too, for Tom had cheered them on. I ran to the edge of the lawn and saw a steep slope leading to the sands and the sea. Now I knew what the sea was, for after Tom had shot me in the back I lived by it for a long while, and once swam across a little creek to get to my form, from which it cut me off.

While I ran down that slope fast as my aching legs would carry me, I made up my mind that I would swim out into the sea and drown there, since it is better to drown than to be torn to pieces.

*   *   *

"Why are you laughing, friend Mahatma."

"I am not laughing," I said. "In this state, without a body, I have nothing to laugh with. Still you are right, for you see that I should be laughing if I could. Your story of the stout lady and the dogs and the china is very amusing."

"Perhaps, friend, but it did not amuse me. Nothing is amusing when one is going to be eaten alive."

"Of course it isn't," I answered. "Please forgive me and go on."

*   *   *

"Well, I tumbled down that cliff, followed by some of the dogs and Tom and the girl Ella and the huntsman Jerry on foot, and dragged myself across the sands till I came to the lip of the sea.

Just here there was a boat and by it stood Giles the keeper. He had come there to get out of the way of the hunting, which he hated as much as he did the coursing. The sight of him settled me—into the sea I went. The dogs wanted to follow me, but Jerry called and whipped them off.

"I won't have them caught in the current and drowned," he said. "Let the flea-bitten old devil go, she's brought trouble enough already."

"Help me shove off the boat, Giles," shouted Tom. "She shan't beat us; we must have her for the hounds. Come on, Ella."

"Best leave her alone, Master Tom," said Giles. "I think she's an unlucky one, that I do."

Still the end of it was that he helped to float the little boat and got into it with Tom and Ella.

Just after they had pushed off I saw a man running down the steps on the cliff waving his arms while he called out something. But of him they took no heed. I do not think they noticed him. As for me, I swam on.

I could not go very fast because I was so dreadfully tired; also I did not like swimming, and the cold waves broke over my head, making the cut in my nose smart and filling my eyes with something that stung them. I could not see far either, nor did I know where I was going. I knew nothing except I was about to die, and that soon everything would be at an end; men, dogs—everything, yes, even Tom. I wanted things to come to an end. I had suffered so dreadfully, life was so horrible, I was so very tired. I felt that it was better to die and have done.

So I swam on a long way and began to forget things; indeed I thought that I was playing in the big turnip field with my mother and sister. But just as I was sinking exhausted a hand shot down into the water and caught me by the ears, although from below the fingers looked as though they were bending away from me. I saw it coming and tried to sink more quickly, but could not.

"I've got her," said the voice of Tom gleefully. "My! Isn't she a beauty? Over nine pounds if she is an ounce. Only just in time, though," he went on, "for, look! She's drowning; her head wobbles as though she were sea-sick. Buck up, pussie, buck up! You mustn't cheat the hounds at last, you know. It wouldn't be sportsmanlike, and they hate dead hares."

Then he held me by my hind legs to drain the water out of me, and afterwards began to blow down my nose, I did not know why.

"Don't do that, Tom," said Ella sharply. "It's nasty."

"Must keep the life in her somehow," answered Tom, and went on blowing.

"Master Tom," interrupted Giles, who was rowing the boat. "I ain't particular, but I wish you'd leave that there hare alone. Somehow I thinks there's bad news in its eye. Who knows? P'raps the little devil feels. Any way, it's a rum one, its swimming out to sea. I never see'd a hunted hare do that afore."

"Bosh!" said Tom, and continued his blowing.

We reached the shore and Tom jumped out of the boat, holding me by the ears. The hounds were all on the beach, most of them lying down, for they were very tired, but the men were standing in a knot at a distance talking earnestly, Tom ran to the hounds, crying out—

"Here she is, my beauties, here she is!" whereon they got up and began to bay. Then he held me above them.

"Master Tom," I heard Jerry's voice say, "for God's sake let that hare go and listen, Master Tom," and the girl Ella, who of a sudden had begun to sob, tried to pull him back.

But he was mad to see me bitten to death and eaten, and until he had done so would attend to no one. He only shouted, "One—two—three! Now, hounds! Worry, worry, worry!"

Then he threw me into the air above the red throats and gnashing teeth which leapt up towards me.

*   *   *

The Hare paused, but added, "Did you tell me, friend Mahatma, that you had never been torn to pieces by hounds, 'broken up,' I believe they call it?"

"Yes, I did," I answered, "and what is more I shall be obliged if you will not dwell upon the subject."

THE COMING OF THE RED-FACED MAN

"As you like," said the Hare. "Certainly it was very dreadful. It seemed to last a long time. But I don't mind it so much now, for I feel that it can never happen to me again. At least I hope it can't, for I don't know what I have done to deserve such a fate, any more than I know why it should have happened to me once."

"Something you did in a previous existence, perhaps," I answered. "You see then you may have hunted other creatures so cruelly that at last your turn came to suffer what you had made them suffer. I often think that because of what we have done before we men are also really being hunted by something we cannot see."

"Ah!" exclaimed the Hare, "I never thought of that. I hope it is true, for it makes things seem juster and less wicked. But I say, friend Mahatma, what am I doing here now, where you tell me poor creatures with four feet never, or hardly ever come?"

"I don't know, Hare. I am not wise, to whom it is only

granted to visit the Road occasionally to search for someone."

"I understand, Mahatma, but still you must know a great deal or you would not be allowed in such a place before your time, or at any rate you must be able to guess a great deal. So tell me, why do you think that I am here?"

"I can't say, Hare, I can't indeed. Perhaps after the Gates are open and your Guardian has given you to drink of the Cup, you will go to sleep and wake up again as something else."

"To drink of the cup, Mahatma? I don't drink; at least I didn't, though I can't tell what may happen here. But what do you mean about waking up as something else? Please be more plain. As what else?"

"Oh! Who can know? Possibly as you are on the human Road you might even become a man some day, though I should not advise you to build on such a hope as that."

"What do you say, Mahatma? A man! One of those two-legged beasts that hunt hares; a thing like Giles and Tom—yes, Tom? Oh! Not that—not that! I'd almost rather go through everything again than become a cruel, torturing man."

As it spoke thus the Hare grew so disturbed that it nearly vanished; literally it seemed to melt away till I could only perceive its outline. With a kind of shock I comprehended all the horror that it must feel at such a prospect as I had suggested to it, and really this grasping of the truth hurt my human pride. It had never come home to me before that the circumstances of their lives—and deaths—must cause some creatures to see us in strange lights.

"Oh! I have no doubt I was mistaken," I said hurriedly, "and that your wishes on the point will be respected. I told you that I know nothing."

At these words the Hare became quite visible again.

It sat up and very reflectively began to rub its still shadowy nose with a shadowy paw. I think that it remembered the sting of the salt water in the cut made by the glass of the window through which it had sprung.

Believing that its remarkable story was done, and that presently it would altogether melt away and vanish out of my knowledge, I looked about me. First I looked above the towering Gates to see whether the Lights had yet begun to change. Then as they had not I looked down the Great White Road, following it for miles and miles, until even to my spirit sight it lost itself in the Nowhere.

Presently coming up this Road towards us I saw a man dressed in a green coat, riding-breeches and boots and a peaked cap, who held in his hand a hunting-whip. He was a fine-looking person of middle age, with a pleasant, open countenance, bright blue eyes, and very red cheeks, on which he wore light-coloured whiskers. In short a jovial-looking individual, with whom things had evidently always gone well, one to whom sorrow and disappointment and mental struggle were utter strangers. He, at least, had never known what it is to "endure hardness" in all his life.

Studying his nature as one can do on the Road, I perceived also that in him there was no guile. He was a good-minded, God-fearing man according to his simple lights, who had done many kindnesses and contributed liberally towards the wants of the poor, though as he had been very rich, it had cost him little thus to gratify the natural promptings of his heart.

Moreover he was what Jorsen calls a "young soul," quite young indeed, by which I mean that he had not often walked the Road in previous states of life, as for instance that Eastern woman had done who accosted me before the arrival of the Hare. So to speak his crude nature had scarcely outgrown the primitive human condition in which necessity as well as taste make it customary and pleasant to men to kill; that condition through which almost every boy passes on his way to manhood, I suppose by the working of some secret law of reminiscence.

It was this thought that first led me to connect the new-comer with the Red-faced Man of the Hare's story. It may seem strange that I should have been so dense, but the truth is that it never occurred to me, any more than it had done to the Hare, that such a person would be at all likely to tread the Road for many years to come. I had gathered that he was comparatively young, and although I had argued otherwise with the Hare, had concluded therefore that he would continue to live his happy earth life until old age brought him to a natural end. Hence my obtuseness.

The man was drifting towards me thoughtfully, evidently much bewildered by his new surroundings but not in the least afraid. Indeed there none are afraid; when they glide from their death-beds to the Road they leave fear behind them with the other terrors of our mortal lot.

Presently he became conscious of the presence of the Hare, and thoughts passed through his mind which of course I could read.

"My word!" he said to himself, "things are better than I hoped. There's a hare, and where there are hares there must be hunting and shooting. Oh! If only I had a gun, or the ghost of a gun!"

Then an idea struck him. He lifted his hunting-crop and hurled it at the Hare.

As it was only the shadow of a crop of course it could hurt nothing. Still it went through the shadow of the Hare and caused it to twist round like lightning.

"That was a good shot anyway," he reflected, with a satisfied smile.

By now the Hare had seen him.

"The Red-faced Man!" it exclaimed, "Grampus himself!" and it turned to flee away.

"Don't be frightened," I cried, "he can't hurt you; nothing can hurt you here."

The Hare halted and sat up. "No," it said, "I forgot. But you saw, he tried to. Now, Mahatma, you will understand what a bloodthirsty brute he is. Even after I am dead he has tried to kill me again."

"Well, and why not?" interrupted the Man. "What are hares for except to be killed?"

"There, Mahatma, you hear him. Look at me, Man, who am

I?"

So he looked at the Hare and the Hare looked at him. Presently his face grew puzzled.

"By Jingo!" he said slowly, "you are uncommonly like—you *are* that accursed witch of a hare which cost me my life. There are the white marks on your back, and there is the grey splotch on your ear. Oh! If only I had a gun—a real gun!"

"You would shoot me, wouldn't you, or try to?" said the Hare. "Well, you haven't and you can't. You say I cost you your life. What do you mean? It was my life that was sacrificed, not yours."

"Indeed," answered the Man, "I thought you got away. Never saw any more of you after you jumped through the French window. Never had time. The last thing I remember is her Ladyship screaming like a mad cockatoo, yes, and abusing me as though I were a pickpocket, with the drawing-room all on fire. Then something happened, and down I went among the broken china and hit my head against the leg of a table. Next came a kind of whirling blackness and I woke up here."

"A fit or a stroke," I suggested.

"Both, I think, sir. The fit first—I have had 'em before, and the stroke afterwards—against the leg of the table. Anyway they finished me between them, thanks to that little beast."

Then it was that I saw a very strange thing, a hare in a rage. It seemed to go mad, of course I mean spiritually mad. Its eyes flashed fire; it opened its mouth and shut it after the fashion of a suffocating fish. At last it spoke in its own way—I cannot stop to explain in further detail the exact manner of speech or rather of its equivalent upon the Road.

"Man, Man," it exclaimed, "you say that I finished you. But what did you do to me? You shot me. Look at the marks upon my back. You coursed me with your running dogs. You hunted me with your hounds. You dragged me out of the sea into which I swam to escape you by death, and threw me living to the pack," and the Hare stopped exhausted by its own fury.

"Well," replied the Man coolly, "and suppose I, or my people, did, what of it? Why shouldn't I? You were a beast, I was a man with dominion over you. You can read all about that in the Book of Genesis."

"I never heard of the Book of Genesis," said the Hare, "but what does dominion mean? Does this Book of Genesis say that it means the right to torment that which is weaker than the tormentor?"

"All you animals were made for us to eat," commented the Man, avoiding an answer to the direct question.

"Very good," answered the Hare, "let us suppose that we *were* given you to eat. Was it in order to eat me that you came out against me with guns, then with dogs that run by sight, and then with dogs that run by smell?"

"If you were to be killed and eaten, why should you not be killed in one of these ways, Hare?"

"Why should I be killed in those ways, Man, when others more merciful were to your hand? Indeed, why should I be killed at all? Moreover, if you wished to satisfy your hunger with my body, why at the last was I thrown to the dogs to devour?"

"I don't quite know, Hare. Never looked at the matter in that light before. But—ah! I've got you now," he added triumphantly. "If it hadn't been for me you never would have lived. You see *I* gave you the gift of life. Therefore, instead of grumbling, you should be very much obliged to me. Don't you understand? I preserved hares, so that without me you would never have been a hare. Isn't that right, Mr.— Mr.—I am sorry I have forgotten your name," he added, turning towards me.

"Mahatma," I said.

"Oh! Yes, I remember it now—Mr.—ah—Mr. Hatter."

"There is something in the argument," I replied cautiously, "but let us hear our friend's answer."

"Answer—my answer! Well, here it is. What are you, Man, who dare to say that you give life or withhold it? You a Lord of life, *you!* I tell you that I know little, yet I am sure that you or those like you have no more power to create life than the world we have left has to bid the stars to shine. If the life must come, it will come, and if it cannot fulfil itself as a hare, then it will appear as something else. If you say that you create life, I, the poor beast which you tortured, tell you that you are a presumptuous liar."

"You dare to lecture me," said the Man, "me, the heir of all the ages, as the poet called me. Why, you nasty little animal, do you know that I have killed hundreds like you, and," he added, with a sudden afflatus of pride, "thousands of other creatures, such as pheasants, to say nothing of deer and larger game? That has been my principal occupation since I was a boy. I may say that I have lived for sport; got very little else to show for my life, so to speak."

"Oh!" said the Hare, "have you? Well, if I were you, I shouldn't boast about it just now. You see, we are still outside of those Gates. Who knows but that you will find every one of the living things you have amused yourself by slaughtering waiting for you within them, each praying for justice to its Maker and your own?"

"My word!" said the Man, "what a horrible notion; it's like a bad dream."

He reflected a little, then added, "Well, if they do, I've got my answer. I killed them for food; man must live. Millions of pheasants are sold to be eaten every year at a much smaller price than they cost to breed. What do you say to that, Mr. Hatter? Finishes him, I think."

"I'm not arguing," I replied. "Ask the Hare."

"Yes, ask me, Man, and although you are repeating yourself, I'll answer with another question, knowing that here you must tell the truth. Did you really rear us all for food? Was it for this that you kept your keepers, your running dogs and your hunting dogs, that you might kill poor defenceless beasts and birds to fill men's stomachs? If this was so, I have nothing more to say. Indeed, if our deaths or sufferings at their hands really help men in any way, I have nothing more to say. I admit that you are higher and stronger than we are, and have a right to use us for your own advantage, or even to destroy us altogether if we harm you."

The Man pondered, then replied sullenly—

"You know very well that it was not so. I did not rear up pheasants and hares merely to eat them or that others might eat them. Something forces me to tell you that it was in order that I might enjoy myself by showing my skill in shooting them, or to have the pleasure and exercise of hunting them to death. Still," he added defiantly, "I who am a Christian man maintain that my religion perfectly justified me in doing all these things, and that no blame attaches to me on this account."

"Very good," said the Hare, "now we have a clear issue. Friend Mahatma, when those Gates open presently what happens beyond them?"

"I don't know," I answered, "I have never been there; at least not that I can remember."

"Still, friend Mahatma, is it not said that yonder lives some Power which judges righteously and declares what is true and what is false?"

"I have heard so, Hare."

"Very well, Man, I lay my cause before that Power—do you the same. If I am wrong I will go back to earth to be tortured by you and yours again. If, however, I am right, you shall abide the judgment of the Power, and I ask that It will make of you—a hunted hare!"

Now when he heard these awful words—for they were awful—no less, the Red-faced Man grew much disturbed. He hummed and he hawed, and shifted his feet about. At last he said—

"You must admit that while you lived you had a first-class time under my protection. Lots of turnips to eat and so forth."

"A first-class time!" the Hare answered with withering scorn. "What sort of a time would you have had if someone had shot you all over the back and you must creep away to die of pain and starvation? How would you have enjoyed it if, from day to day, you had been forced to live in terror of cunning monsters, who at any hour might appear to hurt you in some new fashion?

Do you suppose that animals cannot feel fear, and is continual fear the kind of friend that gives them a 'first-class time'?"

To this last argument the Man seemed able to find no answer.

"Mr. Hare," he said humbly, "we are all fallible. Although I never thought to find myself in the position of having to do so, I will admit that I may possibly have been mistaken in my views and treatment of you and your kind, and indeed of other creatures. If so, I apologise for any, ah—temporary inconvenience I may have caused you. I can do no more."

"Come, Hare," I interposed, "that's handsome; perhaps you might let bygones be bygones."

"Apologise!" exclaimed the Hare. "After all I have suffered I do not think it is enough. At the very least, Mahatma, he should say that he is heartily ashamed and sorry."

"Well, well," said the Man, "it's no use making two bites of a cherry. I am sorry, truly sorry for all the pain and terror I have brought on you. If that won't do let's go up and settle the matter, and if I've been wrong I'll try to bear the consequences like a gentleman. Only, Mr. Hare, I hope that you will not wish to put your case more strongly against me than you need."

"Not I, Man. I know now that you only erred because the truth had not been revealed to you—because you did not understand. All that I will ask, if I can, is that you may be allowed to tell this truth to other men."

"Well, I am glad to say I can't do that, Hare."

"Don't be so sure," I broke in; "it's just the kind of thing which might be decreed—a generation or two hence when the world is fit to listen to you."

But he took no heed, or did not comprehend me, and went on—

"It is an impossibility, and if I did they would think me a lunatic or a snivelling, sentimental humbug. I believe that lots of my old friends would scarcely speak to me again. Why, putting aside the pleasures of sport, if the views you preach were to be accepted, what would become of keepers and beaters and huntsmen and dog-breeders, and of thousands of others who directly or indirectly get their living out of hunting and shooting? Where would game rents be also?"

"I don't know, I am sure," replied the Hare wearily. "I suppose that they would earn their living in some other way, as they must in countries where there is no sport, and that you would have to make up for shooting rents by growing more upon the land. You know that after all we hares and the other game eat a great deal which might be saved if there were not so many of us. But I am not wise, and I have never looked at the question from that point of view. It may seem selfish, but I have to consider myself and the creatures whose cause I plead, for something inside me is telling me now—yes, now—that all of them are speaking through my mouth. It says that is why I am allowed to be here and to talk with you both; for their sakes rather than for my own."

"If you have more to say you had better say it quickly," I interrupted, addressing the Red-faced Man. "I see that the Lights are beginning to change, which means that soon the Road will be closed and the Gates opened."

"I can't remember anything," he answered. "Yes, there is one matter," he added nervously. "I see, Mr. Hare, that you are thinking of my boy Tom, not very kindly I am afraid. As you have been so good as to forgive me I hope that you won't be hard on Tom. He is not at all a bad sort of a lad if a little thoughtless, like many other young people."

"I don't like Tom," said the Hare, with decision. "Tom shot me when you told him not to shoot. Tom shut me up in a filthy place with a yellow rabbit which he forgot to feed, so that it wanted to eat me. Tom tried to cut me off from the wood so that the running dogs might catch me, although you shouted to him that it was not sportsmanlike. Tom dragged me out of the sea and blew down my nostrils to keep me alive. Tom threw me to the hounds, although Giles remonstrated with him and even the huntsman begged him to let me go. I tell you that I don't like Tom."

"Still, Mr. Hare," pleaded the Red-faced Man, "I hope that if it should be in your power when we get through those Gates, that you will be merciful to Tom. I can't think of much to say for him in this hurry, but there, he is my only son and the truth is that I love him. You know he may live—to be different—if you don't bring some misfortune on him."

"Who am I to bring misfortune or to withhold it?" asked the Hare, softening visibly. "Well, I know what love means, for my mother loved me and I loved her in my way. I tell you that when I saw her dead, turned from a beautiful living thing into a stained lump of flesh and fur, I felt dreadful. I understand now that you love Tom as my mother loved me, and, Man, for the sake of your love—not for his sake, mind —I promise you that I won't say anything against Tom if I can help it, or do anything either."

"You're a real good fellow!" exclaimed the Red-faced Man, with evident relief. "Give me your hand. Oh! I forgot, you can't. Hullo! What's up now? Everything seems to be altering."

*   *   *

As he spoke, to my eyes the Lights began to change in earnest. All the sky (I call it sky for clearness) above the mighty Gates became as it were alive with burning tongues of every colour that an artist can conceive. By degrees these fiery tongues or swords shaped themselves into a vast circle which drove back the walls of darkness, and through this circle, guided, guarded by the spirits of dead suns, with odours and with chantings, descended that crowned City of the Mansions before whose glory imagination breaks and even Vision veils her eyes.

It descended, its banners wavering in the winds of prayer; it hung above the Gates, the flowers of all splendours, Heaven's very rose, hung like an opal on the boundless breast of night, and there it stayed.

The Voice in the North called to the Voice in the South; the Voice in the East called to the Voice in the West, and up the Great White Road sped the Angel of the Road, making report as he came that all his multitude were gathered in and for that while the Road was barred.

He passed and in a flash the Gates were burned away. The ashes of them fell upon the heads of those waiting at the Gates, whitening their faces and drying their tears before the Change. They fell upon the Man and the Hare beside me, veiling them as it were and making them silent, but on me they did not fall. Then, from between the Wardens of the Gates, flowed forth the Helpers and the Guardians (save those who already were without comforting the children) seeking their beloved and bearing the Cups of slumber and new birth; then pealed the question—

"Who hath suffered most? Let that one first taste of peace."

Now all the dim hosts surged forward since each outworn soul believed that it had suffered most and was in the bitterest need of peace. But the Helpers and the Guardians gently pressed them back, and again there pealed, no question but a command.

This was the command:

"Draw near, thou Hare."

*   *   *

Jorsen asked me what happened after this justification of the Hare, which, if I heard aright, appeared to suggest that by the decree of some judge unknown, the woes of such creatures are not unnoted and despised, or left unsolaced. Of course I had to answer him that I could not tell.

Perhaps nothing happened at all. Perhaps all the wonders I seemed to see, even the Road by which souls travel from There to Here and from Here to There, and the Gates that were burned away, and the City of the Mansions that descended, were but signs and symbols of mysteries which as yet we cannot grasp or understand.

Whatever may be the truth as to this matter of my visions, I need hardly add, however, that no one can be more anxious than I am myself to learn in what way the Red-faced Man, speaking on behalf of our dominant race, and the Hare, speaking as an appointed advocate of the subject animal creation, finished their argument in the light of fuller knowledge. Much also do I wonder which of them was proved to be right, a difficult matter whereon I feel quite incompetent to express any views.

But you see at that moment I woke up. The edge of the Road on which I was standing seemed to give way beneath me, and I fell into space as one does in a nightmare. It is a very unpleasant sensation.

*   *   *

I remember noticing afterwards that I could not have been long asleep. When I began to dream I had only just blown out the candle, and when I awoke again there was still a smouldering spark upon its wick.

But, as I have said, in that spirit-land wither I had journeyed is to be found neither time nor space nor any other familiar thing.

BLACK HEART AND WHITE HEART: A ZULU IDYLL

CHAPTER I

PHILIP HADDEN AND KING CETYWAYO

At the date of our introduction to him, Philip Hadden was a transport-rider and trader in "the Zulu." Still on the right side of forty, in appearance he was singularly handsome; tall, dark, upright, with keen eyes, short-pointed beard, curling hair and clear-cut features. His life had been varied, and there were passages in it which he did not narrate even to his most intimate friends. He was of gentle birth, however, and it was said that he had received a public school and university education in England. At any rate he could quote the classics with aptitude on occasion, an accomplishment which, coupled with his refined voice and a bearing not altogether common in the wild places of the world, had earned for him among his rough companions the *soubriquet* of "The Prince."

However these things may have been, it is certain that he had emigrated to Natal under a cloud, and equally certain that his relatives at home were content to take no further interest in his fortunes. During the fifteen or sixteen years which he had spent in or about the colony, Hadden followed many trades, and did no good at any of them. A clever man, of agreeable and prepossessing manner, he always found it easy to form friendships and to secure a fresh start in life. But, by degrees, the friends were seized with a vague distrust of him; and, after a period of more or less application, he himself would close the opening that he had made by a sudden disappearance from the locality, leaving behind him a doubtful reputation and some bad debts.

Before the beginning of this story of the most remarkable episodes in his life, Philip Hadden was engaged for several years in transport-riding—that is, in carrying goods on ox waggons from Durban or Maritzburg to various points in the interior. A difficulty such as had more than once confronted him in the course of his career, led to his temporary abandonment of this means of earning a livelihood. On arriving at the little frontier town of Utrecht in the Transvaal, in charge of two waggon loads of mixed goods consigned to a storekeeper there, it was discovered that out of six cases of brandy five were missing from his waggon. Hadden explained the matter by throwing the blame upon his Kaffir "boys," but the storekeeper, a rough-tongued man, openly called him a thief and refused to pay the freight on any of the load. From words the two men came to blows, knives were drawn, and before anybody could interfere the storekeeper received a nasty wound in his side. That night, without waiting till the matter could be inquired into by the landdrost or magistrate, Hadden slipped away, and trekked back into Natal as quickly as his oxen would travel. Feeling that even here he was not safe, he left one of his waggons at Newcastle, loaded up the other with Kaffir goods—such as blankets, calico, and hardware—and crossed into Zululand, where in those days no sheriff's officer would be likely to follow him.

Being well acquainted with the language and customs of the natives, he did good trade with them, and soon found himself possessed of some cash and a small herd of cattle, which he received in exchange for his wares. Meanwhile news reached him that the man whom he had injured still vowed vengeance against him, and was in communication with the authorities in Natal. These reasons making his return to civilisation undesirable for the moment, and further business being impossible until he could receive a fresh supply of trade stuff, Hadden like a wise man turned his thoughts to pleasure. Sending his cattle and waggon over the border to be left in charge of a native headman with whom he was friendly, he went on foot to Ulundi to obtain permission from the king, Cetywayo, to hunt game in his country. Somewhat to his surprise, the Indunas or headmen, received him courteously—for Hadden's visit took place within a few months of the outbreak of the Zulu war in 1878, when Cetywayo was already showing unfriendliness to the English traders and others, though why the king did so they knew not.

On the occasion of his first and last interview with Cetywayo, Hadden got a hint of the reason. It happened thus. On the second morning after his arrival at the royal kraal, a messenger came to inform him that "the Elephant whose tread shook the earth" had signified that it was his pleasure to see him. Accordingly he was led through the thousands of huts and across the Great Place to the little enclosure where Cetywayo, a royal-looking Zulu seated on a stool, and wearing a kaross of leopard skins, was holding an *indaba*, or conference, surrounded by his counsellors. The Induna who had conducted him to the august presence went down upon his hands and knees, and, uttering the royal salute of *Bayéte*, crawled forward to announce that the white man was waiting.

"Let him wait," said the king angrily; and, turning, he continued the discussion with his counsellors.

Now, as has been said, Hadden thoroughly understood Zulu; and, when from time to time the king raised his voice, some of the words he spoke reached his ear.

"What!" Cetywayo said, to a wizened and aged man who seemed to be pleading with him earnestly; "am I a dog that these white hyenas should hunt me thus? Is not the land mine, and was it not my father's before me? Are not the people mine to save or to slay? I tell you that I will stamp out these little white men; my *impis* shall eat them up. I have said!"

Again the withered aged man interposed, evidently in the character of a peacemaker. Hadden could not hear his talk, but he rose and pointed towards the sea, while from his expressive gestures and sorrowful mien, he seemed to be prophesying disaster should a certain course of action be followed.

For a while the king listened to him, then he sprang from his seat, his eyes literally ablaze with rage.

"Hearken," he cried to the counsellor; "I have guessed it for long, and now I am sure of it. You are a traitor. You are

Sompseu's[5] dog, and the dog of the Natal Government, and I will not keep another man's dog to bite me in my own house. Take him away!"

A slight involuntary murmur rose from the ring of *indunas*, but the old man never flinched, not even when the soldiers, who presently would murder him, came and seized him roughly. For a few seconds, perhaps five, he covered his face with the corner of the kaross he wore, then he looked up and spoke to the king in a clear voice.

"O King," he said, "I am a very old man; as a youth I served under Chaka the Lion, and I heard his dying prophecy of the coming of the white man. Then the white men came, and I fought for Dingaan at the battle of the Blood River. They slew Dingaan, and for many years I was the counsellor of Panda, your father. I stood by you, O King, at the battle of the Tugela, when its grey waters were turned to red with the blood of Umbulazi your brother, and of the tens of thousands of his people. Afterwards I became your counsellor, O King, and I was with you when Sompseu set the crown upon your head and you made promises to Sompseu—promises that you have not kept. Now you are weary of me, and it is well; for I am very old, and doubtless my talk is foolish, as it chances to the old. Yet I think that the prophecy of Chaka, your great-uncle, will come true, and that the white men will prevail against you and that through them you shall find your death. I would that I might have stood in one more battle and fought for you, O King, since fight you will, but the end which you choose is for me the best end. Sleep in peace, O King, and farewell. *Bayéte!*"[6]

For a space there was silence, a silence of expectation while men waited to hear the tyrant reverse his judgment. But it did not please him to be merciful, or the needs of policy outweighed his pity.

5 Sir Theophilus Shepstone's.
6 The royal salute of the Zulus.

"Take him away," he repeated. Then, with a slow smile on his face and one word, "Good-night," upon his lips, supported by the arm of a soldier, the old warrior and statesman shuffled forth to the place of death.

Hadden watched and listened in amazement not unmixed with fear. "If he treats his own servants like this, what will happen to me?" he reflected. "We English must have fallen out of favour since I left Natal. I wonder whether he means to make war on us or what? If so, this isn't my place."

Just then the king, who had been gazing moodily at the ground, chanced to look up. "Bring the stranger here," he said.

Hadden heard him, and coming forward offered Cetywayo his hand in as cool and nonchalant a manner as he could command.

Somewhat to his surprise it was accepted. "At least, White Man," said the king, glancing at his visitor's tall spare form and cleanly cut face, "you are no 'umfagozan' (low fellow); you are of the blood of chiefs."

"Yes, King," answered Hadden, with a little sigh, "I am of the blood of chiefs."

"What do you want in my country, White Man?"

"Very little, King. I have been trading here, as I daresay you have heard, and have sold all my goods. Now I ask your leave to hunt buffalo, and other big game, for a while before I return to Natal."

"I cannot grant it," answered Cetywayo, "you are a spy sent by Sompseu, or by the Queen's Induna in Natal. Get you gone."

"Indeed," said Hadden, with a shrug of his shoulders; "then I hope that Sompseu, or the Queen's Induna, or both of them, will pay me when I return to my own country. Meanwhile I will obey you because I must, but I should first like to make you a present."

"What present?" asked the king. "I want no presents. We are rich here, White Man."

"So be it, King. It was nothing worthy of your taking, only a rifle."

"A rifle, White Man? Where is it?"

"Without. I would have brought it, but your servants told me that it is death to come armed before the 'Elephant who shakes the Earth.'"

Cetywayo frowned, for the note of sarcasm did not escape his quick ear.

"Let this white man's offering be brought; I will consider the thing."

Instantly the Induna who had accompanied Hadden darted to the gateway, running with his body bent so low that it seemed as though at every step he must fall upon his face. Presently he returned with the weapon in his hand and presented it to the king, holding it so that the muzzle was pointed straight at the royal breast.

"I crave leave to say, O Elephant," remarked Hadden in a drawling voice, "that it might be well to command your servant to lift the mouth of that gun from your heart."

"Why?" asked the king.

"Only because it is loaded, and at full cock, O Elephant, who probably desires to continue to shake the Earth."

At these words the "Elephant" uttered a sharp exclamation, and rolled from his stool in a most unkingly manner, whilst the terrified Induna, springing backwards, contrived to touch the trigger of the rifle and discharge a bullet through the exact spot that a second before had been occupied by his monarch's head.

"Let him be taken away," shouted the incensed king from the ground, but long before the words had passed his lips the Induna, with a cry that the gun was bewitched, had cast it down and fled at full speed through the gate.

"He has already taken himself away," suggested Hadden, while the audience tittered. "No, King, do not touch it rashly; it is a repeating rifle. Look—" and lifting the Winchester, he fired the four remaining shots in quick succession into the air, striking the top of a tree at which he aimed with every one of them.

"*Wow*, it is wonderful!" said the company in astonishment.

"Has the thing finished?" asked the king.

"For the present it has," answered Hadden. "Look at it."

Cetywayo took the repeater in his hand, and examined it with caution, swinging the muzzle horizontally in an exact line with the stomachs of some of his most eminent Indunas, who shrank to this side and that as the barrel was brought to bear on them.

"See what cowards they are, White Man," said the king with indignation; "they fear lest there should be another bullet in this gun."

"Yes," answered Hadden, "they are cowards indeed. I believe that if they were seated on stools they would tumble off them just as it chanced to your Majesty to do just now."

"Do you understand the making of guns, White Man?" asked the king hastily, while the Indunas one and all turned their heads, and contemplated the fence behind them.

"No, King, I cannot make guns, but I can mend them."

"If I paid you well, White Man, would you stop here at my kraal, and mend guns for me?" asked Cetywayo anxiously.

"It might depend on the pay," answered Hadden; "but for awhile I am tired of work, and wish to rest. If the king gives me the permission to hunt for which I asked, and men to go with me, then when I return perhaps we can bargain on the matter. If not, I will bid the king farewell, and journey to Natal."

"In order to make report of what he has seen and learned here," muttered Cetywayo.

At this moment the talk was interrupted, for the soldiers who had led away the old Induna returned at speed, and prostrated themselves before the king.

"Is he dead?" he asked.

"He has travelled the king's bridge," they answered grimly; "he died singing a song of praise of the king."

"Good," said Cetywayo, "that stone shall hurt my feet no more. Go, tell the tale of its casting away to Sompseu and to the Queen's Induna in Natal," he added with bitter emphasis.

"*Baba!* Hear our Father speak. Listen to the rumbling of the Elephant," said the Indunas taking the point, while one bolder than the rest added: "Soon we will tell them another tale, the white Talking Ones, a red tale, a tale of spears, and the regiments shall sing it in their ears."

At the words an enthusiasm caught hold of the listeners, as the sudden flame catches hold of dry grass. They sprang up, for the most of them were seated on their haunches, and stamping their feet upon the ground in unison, repeated:

Indaba ibomwu—indaba ye mikonto
Lizo dunyiswa nge impi ndhlebeni yaho.
(A red tale! A red tale! A tale of spears,
And the impis *shall sing it in their ears.)*

One of them, indeed, a great fierce-faced fellow, drew near to Hadden and shaking his fist before his eyes—fortunately being in the royal presence he had no assegai—shouted the sentences at him.

The king saw that the fire he had lit was burning too fiercely.

"Silence," he thundered in the deep voice for which he was remarkable, and instantly each man became as if he were turned to stone, only the echoes still answered back: "And the *impis* shall sing it in their ears—in their ears."

"I am growing certain that this is no place for me," thought Hadden; "if that scoundrel had been armed he might have temporarily forgotten himself. Hullo! Who's this?"

Just then there appeared through the gate of the fence a splendid specimen of the Zulu race. The man, who was about thirty-five years of age, was arrayed in a full war dress of a captain of the Umcityu regiment. From the circlet of otter skin on his brow rose his crest of plumes, round his middle, arms and knees hung the long fringes of black oxtails, and in one hand he bore a little dancing shield, also black in colour. The other was empty, since he might not appear before the king bearing arms. In countenance the man was handsome, and though just now they betrayed some anxiety, his eyes were genial and honest, and his mouth sensitive. In height he must have measured six foot two inches, yet he did not strike the observer as being tall, perhaps because of his width of chest and the solidity of his limbs, that were in curious contrast to the delicate and almost womanish hands and feet which so often mark the Zulu of noble blood. In short the man was what he seemed to be, a savage gentleman of birth, dignity and courage.

In company with him was another man plainly dressed in a moocha and a blanket, whose grizzled hair showed him to be over fifty years of age. His face also was pleasant and even refined, but the eyes were timorous, and the mouth lacked character.

"Who are these?" asked the king.

The two men fell on their knees before him, and bowed till their foreheads touched the ground—the while giving him his *sibonga* or titles of praise.

"Speak," he said impatiently.

"O King," said the young warrior, seating himself Zulu fashion, "I am Nahoon, the son of Zomba, a captain of the Umcityu, and this is my uncle Umgona, the brother of one of my mothers, my father's youngest wife."

Cetywayo frowned. "What do you here away from your regiment, Nahoon?"

"May it please the king, I have leave of absence from the head captains, and I come to ask a boon of the king's bounty."

"Be swift, then, Nahoon."

"It is this, O King," said the captain with some embarrassment: "A while ago the king was pleased to make a *keshla* of me because of certain service that I did out yonder—" and he touched the black ring which he wore in the hair of his head. "Being now a ringed man and a captain, I crave the right of a man at the hands of the king— the right to marry."

"Right? Speak more humbly, son of Zomba; my soldiers and my cattle have no rights."

Nahoon bit his lip, for he had made a serious mistake.

"Pardon, O King. The matter stands thus: My uncle Umgona here has a fair daughter named Nanea, whom I desire to wife, and who desires me to husband. Awaiting the king's leave I am betrothed to her and in earnest of it I have paid to Umgona a *lobola* of fifteen head of cattle, cows and calves together. But Umgona has a powerful neighbour, an old chief named Maputa, the warden of the Crocodile Drift, who doubtless is known to the king, and this chief also seeks Nanea in marriage and harries Umgona, threatening him with many evils if he will not give the girl to him. But Umgona's heart is white towards me, and towards Maputa it is black, therefore together we come to crave this boon of the king."

"It is so; he speaks the truth," said Umgona.

"Cease," answered Cetywayo angrily. "Is this a time that my soldiers should seek wives in marriage, wives to turn their hearts to water? Know that but yesterday for this crime I commanded that twenty girls who had dared without my leave to marry men of the Undi regiment, should be strangled and their bodies laid upon the cross-roads and with them the bodies of their fathers, that all might know their sin and be warned thereby. Ay, Umgona, it is well for you and for your daughter that you sought my word before she was given in marriage to this man. Now this is my award: I refuse your prayer, Nahoon, and since you, Umgona, are troubled with one whom you would not take as son-in-law, the old chief Maputa, I will free you from his importunity. The girl, says Nahoon, is fair—good, I myself will be gracious to her, and she shall be numbered among the wives of the royal house. Within thirty days from now, in the week of the next new moon, let her be delivered to the *Sigodhla*, the royal house of the women, and with her those cattle, the cows and the calves together, that Nahoon has given you, of which I fine him because he has dared to think of marriage without the leave of the king."

CHAPTER II

THE BEE PROPHESIES

"'A Daniel come to judgment' indeed," reflected Hadden, who had been watching this savage comedy with interest; "our lovesick friend has got more than he bargained for. Well, that comes of appealing to Cæsar," and he turned to look at the two suppliants.

The old man, Umgona, merely started, then began to pour out sentences of conventional thanks and praise to the king for his goodness and condescension. Cetywayo listened to his talk in silence, and when he had done answered by reminding him tersely that if Nanea did not appear at the date named, both she and he, her father, would in due course certainly decorate a cross-road in their own immediate neighbourhood.

The captain, Nahoon, afforded a more curious study. As the fatal words crossed the king's lips, his face took an expression of absolute astonishment, which was presently replaced by one of fury—the just fury of a man who suddenly has suffered an unutterable wrong. His whole frame quivered, the veins stood out in knots on his neck and forehead, and his fingers closed convulsively as though they were grasping the handle of a spear. Presently the rage passed away—for as well might a man be wroth with fate as with a Zulu despot—to be succeeded by a look of the most hopeless misery. The proud dark eyes grew dull, the copper-coloured face sank in and turned ashen, the mouth drooped, and down one corner of it there trickled a little line of blood springing from the lip bitten through in the effort to keep silence. Lifting his hand in salute to the king, the great man rose and staggered rather than walked towards the gate.

As he reached it, the voice of Cetywayo commanded him to stop. "Stay," he said, "I have a service for you, Nahoon, that shall drive out of your head these thoughts of wives and marriage. You see this white man here; he is my guest, and would hunt buffalo and big game in the bush country. I put him in your charge; take men with you, and see that he comes to no hurt. So also that you bring him before me within a month, or your life shall answer for it. Let him be here at my royal kraal in the first week of the new moon—when Nanea comes—and then I will tell you whether or no I agree with you that she is fair. Go now, my child, and you, White Man, go also; those who are to accompany you shall be with you at the dawn. Farewell, but remember we meet again at the new moon, when we will settle what pay you shall receive as keeper of my guns. Do not fail me, White Man, or I shall send after you, and my messengers are sometimes rough."

"This means that I am a prisoner," thought Hadden, "but it will go hard if I cannot manage to give them the slip somehow. I don't intend to stay in this country if war is declared, to be pounded into *mouti* (medicine), or have my eyes put out, or any little joke of that sort."

*   *   *

Ten days had passed, and one evening Hadden and his escort were encamped in a wild stretch of mountainous country lying between the Blood and Unvunyana Rivers, not more than eight miles from that "Place of the Little Hand" which within a few weeks was to become famous throughout the world by its native name of Isandhlwana. For three days they had been tracking the spoor of a small herd of buffalo that still inhabited the district, but as yet they had not come up with them. The Zulu hunters had suggested that they should follow the Unvunyana down towards the sea where game was more plentiful, but this neither Hadden, nor the captain, Nahoon, had been anxious to do, for reasons which each of them kept secret to himself. Hadden's object was to work gradually down to the Buffalo River across which he hoped to effect a retreat into Natal. That of Nahoon was to linger in the neighbourhood of the kraal of Umgona, which was situated not very far from their present camping place, in the vague hope that he might find an opportunity of speaking with or at least of seeing Nanea, the girl to whom he was affianced, who within a few weeks must be taken from him, and given over to the king.

A more eerie-looking spot than that where they were en-camped Hadden had never seen. Behind them lay a tract of land—half-swamp and half-bush—in which the buffalo were supposed to be hiding. Beyond, in lonely grandeur, rose the mountain of Isandhlwana, while in front was an amphitheatre of the most gloomy forest, ringed round in the distance by sheer-sided hills. Into this forest there ran a river which drained the swamp, placidly enough upon the level. But it was not always level, for within three hundred yards of them it dashed suddenly over a precipice, of no great height but very steep, falling into a boiling rock-bound pool that the light of the sun never seemed to reach.

"What is the name of that forest, Nahoon?" asked Hadden.

"It is named *Emagudu*, The Home of the Dead," the Zulu re-plied absently, for he was looking towards the kraal of Nanea, which was situated at an hour's walk away over the ridge to the right.

"The Home of the Dead! Why?"

"Because the dead live there, those whom we name the *Esemkofu*, the Speechless Ones, and with them other Spirits, the *Amahlosi*, from whom the breath of life has passed away, and who yet live on."

"Indeed," said Hadden, "and have you ever seen these ghosts?"

"Am I mad that I should go to look for them, White Man? Only the dead enter that forest, and it is on the borders of it that our people make offerings to the dead."

Followed by Nahoon, Hadden walked to the edge of the cliff and looked over it. To the left lay the deep and dreadful-looking pool, while close to the bank of it, placed upon a narrow strip of turf between the cliff and the commencement of the forest, was a hut.

"Who lives there?" asked Hadden.

"The great *Isanusi*—she who is named *Inyanga* or Doctor-ess; she who is named Inyosi (the Bee), because she gathers wis-dom from the dead who grow in the forest."

"Do you think that she could gather enough wisdom to tell me whether I am going to kill any buffalo, Nahoon?"

"Mayhap, White Man, but," he added with a little smile, "those who visit the Bee's hive may hear nothing, or they may hear more than they wish for. The words of that Bee have a sting."

"Good; I will see if she can sting me."

"So be it," said Nahoon; and turning, he led the way along the cliff till he reached a native path which zig-zagged down its face.

By this path they climbed till they came to the sward at the foot of the descent, and walked up it to the hut which was surrounded by a low fence of reeds, enclosing a small court-yard paved with ant-heap earth beaten hard and polished. In this court-yard sat the Bee, her stool being placed almost at the mouth of the round opening that served as a doorway to the hut. At first all that Hadden could see of her, crouched as she was in the shadow, was a huddled shape wrapped round with a greasy and tattered catskin kaross, above the edge of which appeared two eyes, fierce and quick as those of a leopard. At her feet smouldered a little fire, and ranged around it in a semi-circle were a number of human skulls, placed in pairs as though they were talking together, whilst other bones, to all appearance also human, were festooned about the hut and the fence of the courtyard.

"I see that the old lady is set up with the usual properties," thought Hadden, but he said nothing.

Nor did the witch-doctoress say anything; she only fixed her beady eyes upon his face. Hadden returned the compliment, staring at her with all his might, till suddenly he became aware that he was vanquished in this curious duel. His brain grew confused, and to his fancy it seemed that the woman before him had shifted shape into the likeness of colossal and horrid spider sitting at the mouth of her trap, and that these bones were the relics of her victims.

"Why do you not speak, White Man?" she said at last in a

slow clear voice. "Well, there is no need, since I can read your thoughts. You are thinking that I who am called the Bee should be better named the Spider. Have no fear; I did not kill these men. What would it profit me when the dead are so many? I suck the souls of men, not their bodies, White Man. It is their living hearts I love to look on, for therein I read much and thereby I grow wise. Now what would you of the Bee, White Man, the Bee that labours in this Garden of Death, and— what brings *you* here, son of Zomba? Why are you not with the Umcityu now that they doctor themselves for the great war—the last war—the war of the white and the black—or if you have no stomach for fighting, why are you not at the side of Nanea the tall, Nanea the fair?"

Nahoon made no answer, but Hadden said:

"A small thing, mother. I would know if I shall prosper in my hunting."

"In your hunting, White Man; what hunting? The hunting of game, of money, or of women? Well, one of them, for a-hunting you must ever be; that is your nature, to hunt and be hunted. Tell me now, how goes the wound of that trader who tasted of your steel yonder in the town of the Maboon (Boers)? No need to answer, White Man, but what fee, Chief, for the poor witch-doctoress whose skill you seek," she added in a whining voice. "Surely you would not that an old woman should work without a fee?"

"I have none to offer you, mother, so I will be going," said Hadden, who began to feel himself satisfied with this display of the Bee's powers of observation and thought-reading.

"Nay," she answered with an unpleasant laugh, "would you ask a question, and not wait for the answer? I will take no fee from you at present, White Man; you shall pay me later on when we meet again," and once more she laughed. "Let me look in your face, let me look in your face," she continued, rising and standing before him.

Then of a sudden Hadden felt something cold at the back of his neck, and the next instant the Bee had sprung from him, holding between her thumb and finger a curl of dark hair which she had cut from his head. The action was so instantaneous that he had neither time to avoid nor to resent it, but stood still staring at her stupidly.

"That is all I need," she cried, "for like my heart my magic is white. Stay—son of Zomba, give me also of your hair, for those who visit the Bee must listen to her humming."

Nahoon obeyed, cutting a little lock from his head with the sharp edge of his assegai, though it was very evident that he did this not because he wished to do so, but because he feared to refuse.

Then the Bee slipped back her kaross, and stood bending over the fire before them, into which she threw herbs taken from a pouch that was bound about her middle. She was still a finely-shaped woman, and she wore none of the abominations which Hadden had been accustomed to see upon the persons of witch-doctoresses. About her neck, however, was a curious ornament, a small live snake, red and grey in hue, which her visitors recognised as one of the most deadly to be found in that part of the country. It is not unusual for Bantu witch-doctors thus to decorate themselves with snakes, though whether or not their fangs have first been extracted no one seems to know.

Presently the herbs began to smoulder, and the smoke of them rose up in a thin, straight stream, that, striking upon the face of the Bee, clung about her head enveloping it as though with a strange blue veil. Then of a sudden she stretched out her hands, and let fall the two locks of hair upon the burning herbs, where they writhed themselves to ashes like things alive. Next she opened her mouth, and began to draw the fumes of the hair and herbs into her lungs in great gulps; while the snake, feeling the influence of the medicine, hissed and, uncoiling itself from about her neck, crept upwards and took refuge among the black *saccaboola* feathers of her head-dress.

Soon the vapours began to do their work; she swayed to and fro muttering, then sank back against the hut, upon the straw of which her head rested. Now the Bee's face was turned upwards towards the light, and it was ghastly to behold, for it had become blue in colour, and the open eyes were sunken like the eyes of one dead, whilst above her forehead the red snake wavered and hissed, reminding Hadden of the Uraeus crest on the brow of statues of Egyptian kings. For ten seconds or more she remained thus, then she spoke in a hollow and unnatural voice:

"O Black Heart and body that is white and beautiful, I look into your heart, and it is black as blood, and it shall be black with blood. Beautiful white body with black heart, you shall find your game and hunt it, and it shall lead you into the House of the Homeless, into the Home of the Dead, and it shall be shaped as a bull, it shall be shaped as a tiger, it shall be shaped as a woman whom kings and waters cannot harm. Beautiful white body and black heart, you shall be paid your wages, money for money, and blow for blow. Think of my word when the spotted cat purrs above your breast; think of it when the battle roars about you; think of it when you grasp your great reward, and for the last time stand face to face with the ghost of the dead in the Home of the Dead.

"O White Heart and black body, I look into your heart and it is white as milk, and the milk of innocence shall save it. Fool, why do you strike that blow? Let him be who is loved of the tiger, and whose love is as the love of a tiger. Ah! What face is that in the battle? Follow it, follow it, O swift of foot; but follow warily, for the tongue that has lied will never plead for mercy, and the hand that can betray is strong in war. White Heart, what is death? In death life lives, and among the dead you shall find the life you lost, for there awaits you she whom kings and waters cannot harm."

As the Bee spoke, by degrees her voice sank lower and lower till it was almost inaudible. Then it ceased altogether and she seemed to pass from trance to sleep. Hadden, who had been listening to her with an amused and cynical smile, now laughed aloud.

"Why do you laugh, White Man?" asked Nahoon angrily.

"I laugh at my own folly in wasting time listening to the nonsense of that lying fraud."

"It is no nonsense, White Man."

"Indeed? Then will you tell me what it means?"

"I cannot tell you what it means yet, but her words have to do with a woman and a leopard, and with your fate and my fate."

Hadden shrugged his shoulders, not thinking the matter worth further argument, and at that moment the Bee woke up shivering, drew the red snake from her head-dress and coiling it about her throat wrapped herself again in the greasy kaross.

"Are you satisfied with my wisdom, *Inkoos*?" she asked of Hadden.

"I am satisfied that you are one of the cleverest cheats in Zululand, mother," he answered coolly. "Now, what is there to pay?"

The Bee took no offence at this rude speech, though for a second or two the look in her eyes grew strangely like that which they had seen in those of the snake when the fumes of the fire made it angry.

"If the white lord says I am a cheat, it must be so," she answered, "for he of all men should be able to discern a cheat. I have said that I ask no fee;—yes, give me a little tobacco from your pouch."

Hadden opened the bag of antelope hide and drawing some tobacco from it, gave it to her. In taking it she clasped his hand and examined the gold ring that was upon the third finger, a ring fashioned like a snake with two little rubies set in the head to represent the eyes.

"I wear a snake about my neck, and you wear one upon your hand, *Inkoos*. I should like to have this ring to wear upon my hand, so that the snake about my neck may be less lonely there."

"Then I am afraid you will have to wait till I am dead," said Hadden.

"Yes, yes," she answered in a pleased voice, "it is a good word. I will wait till you are dead and then I will take the ring, and none can say that I have stolen it, for Nahoon there will bear me witness that you gave me permission to do so."

For the first time Hadden started, since there was something about the Bee's tone that jarred upon him. Had she addressed him in her professional manner, he would have thought nothing of it; but in her cupidity she had become natural, and it was evident that she spoke from conviction, believing her own words.

She saw him start, and instantly changed her note.

"Let the white lord forgive the jest of a poor old witch-doctoress," she said in a whining voice. "I have so much to do with Death that his name leaps to my lips," and she glanced first at the circle of skulls about her, then towards the waterfall that fed the gloomy pool upon whose banks her hut was placed.

"Look," she said simply.

Following the line of her outstretched hand Hadden's eyes fell upon two withered mimosa trees which grew over the fall almost at right angles to its rocky edge. These trees were joined together by a rude platform made of logs of wood lashed down with *riems* of hide. Upon this platform stood three figures; notwithstanding the distance and the spray of the fall, he could see that they were those of two men and a girl, for their shapes stood out distinctly against the fiery red of the sunset sky. One instant there were three, the next there were two—for the girl had gone, and something dark rushing down the face of the fall, struck the surface of the pool with a heavy thud, while a faint and piteous cry broke upon his ear.

"What is the meaning of that?" he asked, horrified and amazed.

"Nothing," answered the Bee with a laugh. "Do you not know, then, that this is the place where faithless women, or girls who have loved without the leave of the king, are brought to meet their death, and with them their accomplices. Oh! They die here thus each day, and I watch them die and keep the count of the number of them," and drawing a tally-stick from the thatch of the hut, she took a knife and added a notch to the many that appeared upon it, looking at Nahoon the while with a half-questioning, half-warning gaze.

"Yes, yes, it is a place of death," she muttered. "Up yonder the quick die day by day and down there"—and she pointed along the course of the river beyond the pool to where the forest began some two hundred yards from her hut—"the ghosts of them have their home. Listen!"

As she spoke, a sound reached their ears that seemed to swell from the dim skirts of the forests, a peculiar and unholy sound which it is impossible to define more accurately than by saying that it seemed beastlike, and almost inarticulate.

"Listen," repeated the Bee, "they are merry yonder."

"Who?" asked Hadden; "the baboons?"

"No, *Inkoos*, the *Amatongo*—the ghosts that welcome her who has just become of their number."

"Ghosts," said Hadden roughly, for he was angry at his own tremors, "I should like to see those ghosts. Do you think that I have never heard a troop of monkeys in the bush before, mother? Come, Nahoon, let us be going while there is light to climb the cliff. Farewell."

"Farewell *Inkoos*, and doubt not that your wish will be fulfilled. Go in peace *Inkoos*—to sleep in peace."

CHAPTER III

THE END OF THE HUNT

The prayer of the Bee notwithstanding, Philip Hadden slept ill that night. He felt in the best of health, and his conscience was not troubling him more than usual, but rest he could not. Whenever he closed his eyes, his mind conjured up a picture of the grim witch-doctoress, so strangely named the Bee, and the sound of her evil-omened words as he had heard them that afternoon. He was neither a superstitious nor a timid man, and any supernatural beliefs that might linger in his mind were, to say the least of it, dormant. But do what he might, he could not shake off a certain eerie sensation of fear, lest there should be some grains of truth in the prophesyings of this hag. What if it were a fact that he was near his death, and that the heart which beat so strongly in his breast must soon be still for ever —no, he would not think of it. This gloomy place, and the dreadful sight which he saw that day, had upset his nerves. The domestic customs of these Zulus were not pleasant, and for his part he was determined to be clear of them so soon as he was able to escape the country.

In fact, if he could in any way manage it, it was his intention to make a dash for the border on the following night. To do this with a good prospect of success, however, it was necessary that he should kill a buffalo, or some other head of game. Then, as he knew well, the hunters with him would feast upon meat until they could scarcely stir, and that would be his opportunity. Nahoon, however, might not succumb to this temptation; therefore he must trust to luck to be rid of him. If it came to the worst, he could put a bullet through him, which he considered he would be justified in doing, seeing that in reality the man was his jailor. Should this necessity arise, he felt indeed that he could face it without undue compunction, for in truth he disliked Nahoon; at times he even hated him. Their natures were antagonistic, and he knew that the great Zulu distrusted and looked down upon him, and to be looked down upon by a savage "nigger" was more than his pride could stomach.

At the first break of dawn Hadden rose and roused his escort, who were still stretched in sleep around the dying fire, each man wrapped in his kaross or blanket. Nahoon stood up and shook himself, looking gigantic in the shadows of the morning.

"What is your will, *Umlungu* (white man), that you are up before the sun?"

"My will, *Muntumpofu* (yellow man), is to hunt buffalo," answered Hadden coolly. It irritated him that this savage should give him no title of any sort.

"Your pardon," said the Zulu reading his thoughts, "but I cannot call you *Inkoos* because you are not my chief, or any man's; still if the title 'white man' offends you, we will give you a name."

"As you wish," answered Hadden briefly.

Accordingly they gave him a name, *Inhlizin-mgama*, by which he was known among them thereafter, but Hadden was not best pleased when he found that the meaning of those soft-sounding syllables was "Black Heart." That was how the *inyanga* had addressed him—only she used different words.

An hour later, and they were in the swampy bush country that lay behind the encampment searching for their game. Within a very little while Nahoon held up his hand, then pointed to the ground. Hadden looked; there, pressed deep in the marshy soil, and to all appearance not ten minutes old, was the spoor of a small herd of buffalo.

"I knew that we should find game to-day," whispered Nahoon, "because the Bee said so."

"Curse the Bee," answered Hadden below his breath. "Come on."

For a quarter of an hour or more they followed the spoor through thick reeds, till suddenly Nahoon whistled very softly and touched Hadden's arm. He looked up, and there, about two hundred yards away, feeding on some higher ground among a patch if mimosa trees, were the buffaloes— six of them—an old bull with a splendid head, three cows, a heifer and a calf about four months old. Neither the wind nor the nature of the veldt were favourable for them to stalk the game from their present position, so they made a detour of half a mile and very carefully crept towards them up the wind, slipping from trunk to trunk of the mimosas and when these failed them, crawling on their stomachs under cover of the tall *tambuti* grass. At last they were within forty yards, and a further advance seemed impracticable; for although he could not smell them, it was evident from his movements that the old bull heard some unusual sound and was growing suspicious. Nearest to Hadden, who alone of the party had a rifle, stood the heifer broadside on—a beautiful shot. Remembering that she would make the best beef, he lifted his Martini, and aiming at her immediately behind the shoulder, gently squeezed the trigger. The rifle exploded, and the heifer fell dead, shot through the heart. Strangely enough the other buffaloes did not at once run away. On the contrary, they seemed puzzled to account for the sudden noise; and, not being able to wind anything, lifted their heads and stared round them.

The pause gave Hadden space to get in a fresh cartridge and to aim again, this time at the old bull. The bullet struck him somewhere in the neck or shoulder, for he came to his knees, but in another second was up and having caught sight of the cloud of smoke he charged straight at it. Because of this smoke, or for some other reason, Hadden did not see him coming, and in consequence would most certainly have been trampled or gored, had not Nahoon sprung forward, at the imminent risk of his own life, and dragged him down behind an ant-heap. A moment more and the great beast had thundered by, taking no further notice of them.

"Forward," said Hadden, and leaving most of the men to cut up the heifer and carry the best of her meat to camp, they started on the blood spoor.

For some hours they followed the bull, till at last they lost the trail on a patch of stony ground thickly covered with bush, and exhausted by the heat, sat down to rest and to eat some *biltong* or sun-dried flesh which they had with them. They finished their meal, and were preparing to return to the camp, when one of the four Zulus who were with them went to drink at a little stream that ran at a distance of not more than ten paces away. Half a minute later they heard a hideous grunting noise and a splashing of water, and saw the Zulu fly into the air. All the while that they were eating, the wounded buffalo had been lying in wait for them under a thick bush on the banks of the streamlet, knowing—cunning brute that he was—that sooner or later his turn would come. With a shout of consternation they rushed forward to see the bull vanish over the rise before Hadden could get a chance of firing at him, and to find their companion dying, for the great horn had pierced his lung.

"It is not a buffalo, it is a devil," the poor fellow gasped, and expired.

"Devil or not, I mean to kill it," exclaimed Hadden. So leaving the others to carry the body of their comrade to camp, he started on accompanied by Nahoon only. Now the ground was more open and the chase easier, for they sighted their quarry frequently, though they could not come near enough to fire. Presently they travelled down a steep cliff.

"Do you know where we are?" asked Nahoon, pointing to a belt of forest opposite. "That is *Emagudu*, the Home of the Dead—and look, the bull heads thither."

Hadden glanced round him. It was true; yonder to the left were the Fall, the Pool of Doom, and the hut of the Bee.

"Very well," he answered; "then we must head for it too."

Nahoon halted. "Surely you would not enter there," he exclaimed.

"Surely I will," replied Hadden, "but there is no need for you to do so if you are afraid."

"I am afraid—of ghosts," said the Zulu, "but I will come."

So they crossed the strip of turf, and entered the haunted wood. It was a gloomy place indeed; the great wide-topped trees grew thick there shutting out the sight of the sky; moreover, the air in it which no breeze stirred, was heavy with the exhalations of rotting foliage. There seemed to be no life here and no sound—only now and again a loathsome spotted snake would uncoil itself and glide away, and now and again a heavy rotten bough fell with a crash.

Hadden was too intent upon the buffalo, however, to be much impressed by his surroundings. He only remarked that the light would be bad for shooting, and went on.

They must have penetrated a mile or more into the forest when the sudden increase of blood upon the spoor told them that the bull's wound was proving fatal to him.

"Run now," said Hadden cheerfully.

"Nay, *hamba gachle*—go softly—" answered Nahoon, "the

devil is dying, but he will try to play us another trick before he dies." And he went on peering ahead of him cautiously.

"It is all right here, anyway," said Hadden, pointing to the spoor that ran straight forward printed deep in the marshy ground.

Nahoon did not answer, but stared steadily at the trunks of two trees a few paces in front of them and to their right. "Look," he whispered.

Hadden did so, and at length made out the outline of something brown that was crouched behind the trees.

"He is dead," he exclaimed.

"No," answered Nahoon, "he has come back on his own path and is waiting for us. He knows that we are following his spoor. Now if you stand there, I think that you can shoot him through the back between the tree trunks."

Hadden knelt down, and aiming very carefully at a point just below the bull's spine, he fired. There was an awful bellow, and the next instant the brute was up and at them. Nahoon flung his broad spear, which sank deep into its chest, then they fled this way and that. The buffalo stood still for a moment, its fore legs straddled wide and its head down, looking first after the one and then the other, till of a sudden it uttered a low moaning sound and rolled over dead, smashing Nahoon's assegai to fragments as it fell.

"There! He's finished," said Hadden, "and I believe it was your assegai that killed him. Hullo! What's that noise?"

Nahoon listened. In several quarters of the forest, but from how far away it was impossible to tell, there rose a curious sound, as of people calling to each other in fear but in no articulate language. Nahoon shivered.

"It is the *Esemkofu*," he said, "the ghosts who have no tongue, and who can only wail like infants. Let us be going; this place is bad for mortals."

"And worse for buffaloes," said Hadden, giving the dead bull a kick, "but I suppose that we must leave him here for your friends, the *Esemkofu*, as we have got meat enough, and can't carry his head."

So they started back towards the open country. As they
threaded their way slowly through the tree trunks, a new idea
came into Hadden's head. Once out of this forest, he was within
an hour's run of the Zulu border, and once over the Zulu border,
he would feel a happier man than he did at that moment. As
has been said, he had intended to attempt to escape in the darkness, but the plan was risky. All the Zulus might not over-eat
themselves and go to sleep, especially after the death of their
comrade; Nahoon, who watched him day and night, certainly
would not. This was his opportunity—there remained the question of Nahoon.

Well, if it came to the worst, Nahoon must die: it would be
easy—he had a loaded rifle, and now that his assegai was gone,
Nahoon had only a kerry. He did not wish to kill the man,
though it was clear to him, seeing that his own safety was at
stake, that he would be amply justified in so doing. Why should
he not put it to him—and then be guided by circumstances?

Nahoon was walking across a little open space about ten
spaces ahead of him where Hadden could see him very well,
whilst he himself was under the shadow of a large tree with low
horizontal branches running out from the trunk.

"Nahoon," he said.

The Zulu turned round, and took a step towards him.

"No, do not move, I pray. Stand where you are, or I shall be
obliged to shoot you. Listen now: do not be afraid for I shall not
fire without warning. I am your prisoner, and you are charged
to take me back to the king to be his servant. But I believe that
a war is going to break out between your people and mine; and
this being so, you will understand that I do not wish to go to
Cetywayo's kraal, because I should either come to a violent
death there, or my own brothers will believe that I am a traitor
and treat me accordingly. The Zulu border is not much more
than an hour's journey away—let us say an hour and a half's: I
mean to be across it before the moon is up. Now, Nahoon, will
you lose me in the forest and give me this hour and a half's

start—or will you stop here with that ghost people of whom you talk? Do you understand? No, please do not move."

"I understand you," answered the Zulu, in a perfectly composed voice, "and I think that was a good name which we gave you this morning, though, Black Heart, there is some justice in your words and more wisdom. Your opportunity is good, and one which a man named as you are should not let fall."

"I am glad to find that you take this view of the matter, Nahoon. And now will you be so kind as to lose me, and to promise not to look for me till the moon is up?"

"What do you mean, Black Heart?"

"What I say. Come, I have no time to spare."

"You are a strange man," said the Zulu reflectively. "You heard the king's order to me: would you have me disobey the order of the king?"

"Certainly, I would. You have no reason to love Cetywayo, and it does not matter to you whether or no I return to his kraal to mend guns there. If you think that he will be angry because I am missing, you had better cross the border also; we can go together."

"And leave my father and all my brethren to his vengeance? Black Heart, you do not understand. How can you, being so named? I am a soldier, and the king's word is the king's word. I hoped to have died fighting, but I am the bird in your noose. Come, shoot, or you will not reach the border before moonrise," and he opened his arms and smiled.

"If it must be, so let it be. Farewell, Nahoon, at least you are a brave man, but every one of us must cherish his own life," answered Hadden calmly.

Then with much deliberation he raised his rifle and covered the Zulu's breast.

Already—whilst his victim stood there still smiling, although a twitching of his lips betrayed the natural terrors that no bravery can banish—already his finger was contracting on the trigger, when of a sudden, as instantly as though he had been struck by lightning, Hadden went down backwards, and behold!

There stood upon him a great spotted beast that waved its long tail to and fro and glared down into his eyes.

It was a leopard—a tiger as they call it in Africa—which, crouched upon a bough of the tree above, had been unable to resist the temptation of satisfying its savage appetite on the man below. For a second or two there was silence, broken only by the purring, or rather the snoring sound made by the leopard. In those seconds, strangely enough, there sprang up before Hadden's mental vision a picture of the *inyanga* called *Inyosi* or the Bee, her death-like head resting against the thatch of the hut, and her death-like lips muttering "think of my word when the great cat purrs above your face."

Then the brute put out its strength. The claws of one paw it drove deep into the muscles of his left thigh, while with another it scratched at his breast, tearing the clothes from it and furrowing the flesh beneath. The sight of the white skin seemed to madden it, and in its fierce desire for blood it drooped its square muzzle and buried its fangs in its victim's shoulder. Next moment there was a sound of running feet and of a club falling heavily. Up reared the leopard with an angry snarl, up till it stood as high as the attacking Zulu. At him it came, striking out savagely and tearing the black man as it had torn the white. Again the kerry fell full on its jaws, and down it went backwards. Before it could rise again, or rather as it was in the act of rising, the heavy knob-stick struck it once more, and with fearful force, this time as it chanced, full on the nape of the neck, and paralysing the brute. It writhed and bit and twisted, throwing up the earth and leaves, while blow after blow was rained upon it, till at length with a convulsive struggle and a stifled roar it lay still— the brains oozing from its shattered skull.

Hadden sat up, the blood running from his wounds.

"You have saved my life, Nahoon," he said faintly, "and I thank you."

"Do not thank me, Black Heart," answered the Zulu, "it was the king's word that I should keep you safely. Still this tiger has been hardly dealt with, for certainly *he* has saved *my* life," and lifting the Martini he unloaded the rifle.

At this juncture Hadden swooned away.

*　　　*　　　*

Twenty-four hours had gone by when, after what seemed to him to be but a little time of troubled and dreamful sleep, through which he could hear voices without understanding what they said, and feel himself borne he knew not whither, Hadden awoke to find himself lying upon a kaross in a large and beautifully clean Kaffir hut with a bundle of furs for a pillow. There was a bowl of milk at his side and tortured as he was by thirst, he tried to stretch out his arm to lift it to his lips, only to find to his astonishment that his hand fell back to his side like that of a dead man. Looking round the hut impatiently, he found that there was nobody in it to assist him, so he did the only thing which remained for him to do—he lay still. He did not fall asleep, but his eyes closed, and a kind of gentle torpor crept over him, half obscuring his recovered senses. Presently he heard a soft voice speaking; it seemed far away, but he could clearly distinguish the words.

"Black Heart still sleeps," the voice said, "but there is colour in his face; I think that he will wake soon, and find his thoughts again."

"Have no fear, Nanea, he will surely wake, his hurts are not dangerous," answered another voice, that of Nahoon. "He fell heavily with the weight of the tiger on top of him, and that is why his senses have been shaken for so long. He went near to death, but certainly he will not die."

"It would have been a pity if he had died," answered the soft voice, "he is so beautiful; never have I seen a white man who was so beautiful."

"I did not think him beautiful when he stood with his rifle pointed at my heart," answered Nahoon sulkily.

"Well, there is this to be said," she replied, "he wished to escape from Cetywayo, and that is not to be wondered at," and she sighed. "Moreover he asked you to come with him, and it might have been well if you had done so, that is, if you would have taken

158

me with you!"

"How could I have done it, girl?" he asked angrily. "Would you have me set at nothing the order of the king?"

"The king!" she replied raising her voice. "What do you owe to this king? You have served him faithfully, and your reward is that within a few days he will take me from you—me, who should have been your wife, and I must—I must—" And she began to weep softly, adding between her sobs, "if you loved me truly, you would think more of me and of yourself, and less of the Black One and his orders. Oh! Let us fly, Nahoon, let us fly to Natal before this spear pierces me."

"Weep not, Nanea," he said; "why do you tear my heart in two between my duty and my love? You know that I am a soldier, and that I must walk the path whereon the king has set my feet. Soon I think I shall be dead, for I seek death, and then it will matter nothing."

"Nothing to you, Nahoon, who are at peace, but to me? Yet, you are right, and I know it, therefore forgive me, who am no warrior, but a woman who must also obey—the will of the king." And she cast her arms about his neck, sobbing her fill upon his breast.

CHAPTER IV

NANEA

Presently, muttering something that the listener could not catch, Nahoon left Nanea, and crept out of the hut by its bee-hole entrance. Then Hadden opened his eyes and looked round him. The sun was sinking and a ray of its red light streaming through the little opening filled the place with a soft and crimson glow. In the centre of the hut— supporting it—stood a thorn-wood roof-tree coloured black by the smoke of the fire; and against this, the rich light falling full upon her, leaned the girl Nanea—a very picture of gentle despair.

As is occasionally the case among Zulu women, she was

beautiful—so beautiful that the sight of her went straight to the white man's heart, for a moment causing the breath to catch in his throat. Her dress was very simple. On her shoulders, hanging open in front, lay a mantle of soft white stuff edged with blue beads, about her middle was a buck-skin moocha, also embroidered with blue beads, while round her forehead and left knee were strips of grey fur, and on her right wrist a shining bangle of copper. Her naked bronze-hued figure was tall and perfect in its proportions; while her face had little in common with that of the ordinary native girl, showing as it did strong traces of the ancestral Arabian or Semitic blood. It was oval in shape, with delicate aquiline features, arched eyebrows, a full mouth, that drooped a little at the corners, tiny ears, behind which the wavy coal-black hair hung down to the shoulders, and the very loveliest pair of dark and liquid eyes that it is possible to imagine.

For a minute or more Nanea stood thus, her sweet face bathed in the sunbeam, while Hadden feasted his eyes upon its beauty. Then sighing heavily, she turned, and seeing that he was awake, started, drew her mantle over her breast and came, or rather glided, towards him.

"The chief is awake," she said in her soft Zulu accents. "Does he need aught?"

"Yes, Lady," he answered; "I need to drink, but alas! I am too weak."

She knelt down beside him, and supporting him with her left arm, with her right held the gourd to his lips.

How it came about Hadden never knew, but before that draught was finished a change passed over him. Whether it was the savage girl's touch, or her strange and fawn-like loveliness, or the tender pity in her eyes, matters not—the issue was the same. She struck some cord in his turbulent uncurbed nature, and of a sudden it was filled full with passion for her—a passion which if, not elevated, at least was real. He did not for a moment mistake the significance of the flood of feeling that surged through his veins. Hadden never shirked facts.

"By Heaven!" he said to himself, "I have fallen in love with a black beauty at first sight—more in love than I have ever been before. It's awkward, but there will be compensations. So much the worse for Nahoon, or for Cetywayo, or for both of them. After all, I can always get rid of her if she becomes a nuisance."

Then, in a fit of renewed weakness, brought about by the turmoil of his blood, he lay back upon the pillow of furs, watching Nanea's face while with a native salve of pounded leaves she busied herself dressing the wounds that the leopard had made.

It almost seemed as though something of what was passing in his mind communicated itself to that of the girl. At least, her hand shook a little at her task, and getting done with it as quickly as she could, she rose from her knees with a courteous "It is finished, *Inkoos*," and once more took up her position by the roof-tree.

"I thank you, Lady," he said; "your hand is kind."

"You must not call me lady, *Inkoos*," she answered, "I am no chieftainess, but only the daughter of a headman, Umgona."

"And named Nanea," he said. "Nay, do not be surprised, I have heard of you. Well, Nanea, perhaps you will soon become a chieftainess—up at the king's kraal yonder."

"Alas! And alas!" she said, covering her face with her hands.

"Do not grieve, Nanea, a hedge is never so tall and thick but that it cannot be climbed or crept through."

She let fall her hands and looked at him eagerly, but he did not pursue the subject.

"Tell me, how did I come here, Nanea?"

"Nahoon and his companions carried you, *Inkoos*."

"Indeed, I begin to be thankful to the leopard that struck me down. Well, Nahoon is a brave man, and he has done me a great service. I trust that I may be able to repay it—to you, Nanea."

*   *   *

This was the first meeting of Nanea and Hadden; but, although she did not seek them, the necessities of his sickness and of the situation brought about many another. Never for a moment did the white man waver in his determination to get into his keeping the native girl who had captivated him, and to attain his end he brought to bear all his powers and charm to detach her from Nahoon, and win her affections for himself. He was no rough wooer, however, but proceeded warily, weaving her about with a web of flattery and attention that must, he thought, produce the desired effect upon her mind. Without a doubt, indeed, it would have done so—for she was but a woman, and an untutored one—had it not been for a simple fact which dominated her whole nature. She loved Nahoon, and there was no room in her heart for any other man, white or black. To Hadden she was courteous and kindly but no more, nor did she appear to notice any of the subtle advances by which he attempted to win a foothold in her heart. For a while this puzzled him, but he remembered that the Zulu women do not usually permit themselves to show feeling towards an undeclared suitor. Therefore it became necessary that he should speak out.

His mind once made up, he had not to wait long for an opportunity. He was now quite recovered from his hurts, and accustomed to walk in the neighbourhood of the kraal. About two hundred yards from Umgona's huts rose a spring, and thither it was Nanea's habit to resort in the evening to bring back drinking-water for the use of her father's household. The path between this spring and the kraal ran through a patch of bush, where on a certain afternoon towards sundown Hadden took his seat under a tree, having first seen Nanea go down to the little stream as was her custom. A quarter of an hour later she reappeared carrying a large gourd upon her head. She wore no garment now except her moocha, for she had but one mantle and was afraid lest the water should splash it. He watched her advancing along the path, her hands resting on her hips, her splendid naked figure outlined against the westering sun, and wondered what excuse he could make to talk with her. As it chanced fortune favoured him, for when she was near him a snake glided across the path in front of the girl's feet, causing her to spring backwards in alarm and overset the gourd of water. He came forward, and picked it up.

"Wait here," he said laughing; "I will bring it to you full."

"Nay, *Inkoos*," she remonstrated, "that is a woman's work."

"Among my people," he said, "the men love to work for the women," and he started for the spring, leaving her wondering.

Before he reached her again, he regretted his gallantry, for it was necessary to carry the handleless gourd upon his shoulder, and the contents of it spilling over the edge soaked him. Of this, however, he said nothing to Nanea.

"There is your water, Nanea, shall I carry it for you to the kraal?"

"Nay, *Inkoos*, I thank you, but give it to me, you are weary with its weight."

"Stay awhile, and I will accompany you. Ah! Nanea, I am still weak, and had it not been for you I think that I should be dead."

"It was Nahoon who saved you—not I, *Inkoos*."

"Nahoon saved my body, but you, Nanea, you alone can save my heart."

"You talk darkly, *Inkoos*."

"Then I must make my meaning clear, Nanea. I love you."

She opened her brown eyes wide.

"You, a white lord, love me, a Zulu girl? How can that be?"

"I do not know, Nanea, but it is so, and were you not blind you would have seen it. I love you, and I wish to take you to wife."

"Nay, *Inkoos*, it is impossible. I am already betrothed."

"Ay," he answered, "betrothed to the king."

"No, betrothed to Nahoon."

"But it is the king who will take you within a week; is it not so? And would you not rather that I should take you than the king?"

"It seems to be so, *Inkoos*, and I would rather go with you than with the king, but most of all I desire to marry Nahoon. It may be that I shall not be able to marry him, but if that is so, at least I will never become one of the king's women."

"How will you prevent it, Nanea?"

"There are waters in which a maid may drown, and trees upon which she can hang," she answered with a quick setting of the mouth.

"That were a pity, Nanea, you are too fair to die."

"Fair or foul, yet I die, *Inkoos*."

"No, no, come with me—I will find a way—and be my wife," and he put her arm about her waist, and strove to draw her to him.

Without any violence of movement, and with the most perfect dignity, the girl disengaged herself from his embrace.

"You have honoured me, and I thank you, *Inkoos*," she said quietly, "but you do not understand. I am the wife of Nahoon—I belong to Nahoon; therefore, I cannot look on any other man while Nahoon lives. It is not our custom, *Inkoos*, for we are not as the white women, but ignorant and simple, and when we vow ourselves to a man, we abide by that vow till death."

"Indeed," said Hadden; "and so now you go to tell Nahoon that I have offered to make you my wife."

"No, *Inkoos*, why should I tell Nahoon your secrets? I have said 'nay' to you, not 'yea,' therefore he has no right to know," and she stooped to lift the gourd of water.

Hadden considered the situation rapidly, for his repulse only made him the more determined to succeed. Of a sudden under the emergency he conceived a scheme, or rather its rough outline. It was not a nice scheme, and some men might have shrunk from it, but as he had no intention of suffering himself to be defeated by a Zulu girl, he decided—with regret, it is true—that having failed to attain his ends by means which he considered fair, he must resort to others of more doubtful character.

"Nanea," he said, "you are a good and honest woman, and I respect you. As I have told you, I love you also, but if you refuse to listen to me there is nothing more to be said, and after all, perhaps it would be better that you should marry one of your own people. But, Nanea, you will never marry him, for the king will take you; and, if he does not give you to some other man, either you will become one of his 'sisters,' or to be free of him, as you say, you will die. Now hear me, for it is because I love you and wish your welfare that I speak thus. Why do you not escape into Natal, taking Nahoon with you, for there as you know you may live in peace out of reach of the arm of Cetywayo?"

"That is my desire, *Inkoos*, but Nahoon will not consent. He says that there is to be war between us and you white men, and he will not break the command of the king and desert from his army."

"Then he cannot love you much, Nahoon, and at least you have to think of yourself. Whisper into the ear of your father and fly together, for be sure that Nahoon will soon follow you. Ay! And I myself with fly with you, for I too believe that there must be war, and then a white man in this country will be as a lamb among the eagles."

"If Nahoon will come, I will go, *Inkoos*, but I cannot fly without Nahoon; it is better I should stay here and kill myself."

"Surely then being so fair and loving him so well, you can teach him to forget his folly and to escape with you. In four days' time we must start for the king's kraal, and if you win over Nahoon, it will be easy for us to turn our faces southwards and across the river that lies between the land of the Amazulu and Natal. For the sake of all of us, but most of all for your own sake, try to do this, Nanea, whom I have loved and whom I now would save. See him and plead with him as you know how, but as yet do not tell him that I dream of flight, for then I should be watched."

"In truth, I will, *Inkoos*," she answered earnestly, "and oh! I thank you for your goodness. Fear not that I will betray you—first would I die. Farewell."

"Farewell, Nanea," and taking her hand he raised it to his lips.

*   *   *

Late that night, just as Hadden was beginning to prepare himself for sleep, he heard a gentle tapping at the board which closed the entrance to his hut.

"Enter," he said, unfastening the door, and presently by the light of the little lantern that he had with him, he saw Nanea creep into the hut, followed by the great form of Nahoon.

"*Inkoos*," she said in a whisper when the door was closed again, "I have pleaded with Nahoon, and he has consented to fly; moreover, my father will come also."

"Is it so, Nahoon?" asked Hadden.

"It is so," answered the Zulu, looking down shamefacedly; "to save this girl from the king, and because the love of her eats out my heart, I have bartered away my honour. But I tell you, Nanea, and you, White Man, as I told Umgona just now, that I think no good will come of this flight, and if we are caught or betrayed, we shall be killed every one of us."

"Caught we can scarcely be," broke in Nanea anxiously, "for who could betray us, except the *Inkoos* here—"

"Which he is not likely to do," said Hadden quietly, "seeing that he desires to escape with you, and that his life is also at stake."

"That is so, Black Heart," said Nahoon, "otherwise I tell you that I should not have trusted you."

Hadden took no notice of this outspoken saying, but until very late that night they sat there together making their plans.

*   *   *

On the following morning Hadden was awakened by sounds of violent altercation. Going out of his hut he found that the disputants were Umgona and a fat and evil-looking Kaffir chief who had arrived at the kraal on a pony. This chief, he soon discovered, was named Maputa, being none other than the man who had sought Nanea in marriage and brought about Nahoon's and Umgona's unfortunate appeal to the king. At present he was engaged in abusing Umgona furiously, charging him with having stolen certain of his oxen and bewitched his cows so that they would not give milk. The alleged theft it was comparatively easy to disprove, but the wizardry remained a matter of argument.

"You are a dog, and a son of a dog," shouted Maputa, shaking his fat fist in the face of the trembling but indignant Umgona. "You promised me your daughter in marriage, then having vowed her to that *umfagozan*—that low lout of a soldier, Nahoon, the son of Zomba—you went, the two of you, and poisoned the king's ear against me, bringing me into trouble with the king, and now you have bewitched my cattle. Well, wait, I will be even with you, Wizard; wait till you wake up in the cold morning to find your fence red with fire, and the slayers standing outside your gates to eat up you and yours with spears—"

At this juncture Nahoon, who till now had been listening in silence, intervened with effect.

"Good," he said, "we will wait, but not in your company, Chief Maputa. *Hamba!* (Go)—" and seizing the fat old ruffian by the scruff of his neck, he flung him backwards with such violence that he rolled over and over down the little slope.

Hadden laughed, and passed on towards the stream where he proposed to bathe. Just as he reached it, he caught sight of Maputa riding along the footpath, his head-ring covered with mud, his lips purple and his black face livid with rage.

"There goes an angry man," he said to himself. "Now, how would it be—" and he looked upwards like one seeking an inspiration. It seemed to come; perhaps the devil finding it open whispered in his ear, at any rate—in a few seconds his plan was formed, and he was walking through the bush to meet Maputa.

"Go in peace, Chief," he said; "they seem to have treated you roughly up yonder. Having no power to interfere, I came away for I could not bear the sight. It is indeed shameful that an old and venerable man of rank should be struck into the dirt, and beaten by a soldier drunk with beer."

"Shameful, White Man!" gasped Maputa; "your words are true indeed. But wait a while. I, Maputa, will roll that stone over, I will throw that bull upon its back. When next the harvest ripens, this I promise, that neither Nahoon nor Umgona, nor any of his kraal shall be left to gather it."

"And how will you manage that, Maputa?"

"I do not know, but I will find a way. Oh! I tell you, a way shall be found."

Hadden patted the pony's neck meditatively, then leaning forward, he looked the chief in the eyes and said:

"What will you give me, Maputa, if I show you that way, a sure and certain one, whereby you may be avenged to the death upon Nahoon, whose violence I also have seen, and upon Umgona, whose witchcraft brought sore sickness upon me?"

"What reward do you seek, White Man?" asked Maputa eagerly.

"A little thing, Chief, a thing of no account, only the girl Nanea, to whom as it chances I have taken a fancy."

"I wanted her for myself, White Man, but he who sits at Ulundi has laid his hand upon her."

"That is nothing, Chief; I can arrange with him who 'sits at Ulundi.' It is with you who are great here that I wish to come to terms. Listen: if you grant my desire, not only will I fulfil yours upon your foes, but when the girl is delivered into my hands I will give you this rifle and a hundred rounds of cartridges."

Maputa looked at the sporting Martini, and his eyes glistened.

"It is good," he said; "it is very good. Often have I wished for such a gun that will enable me to shoot game, and to talk with my enemies from far away. Promise it to me, White Man, and you shall take the girl if I can give her to you."

"You swear it, Maputa?"

"I swear it by the head of Chaka, and the spirits of my fathers."

"Good. At dawn on the fourth day from now it is the purpose of Umgona, his daughter Nanea, and Nahoon, to cross the river into Natal by the drift that is called Crocodile Drift, taking their cattle with them and flying from the king. I also shall be of their company, for they know that I have learned their secret, and would murder me if I tried to leave them. Now you who are chief of the border and guardian of that drift, must hide at night with some men among the rocks in the shallows of the drift and await our coming. First Nanea will cross driving the cows and calves, for so it is arranged, and I shall help her; then will follow Umgona and Nahoon with the oxen and heifers. On these two you must fall, killing them and capturing the cattle, and afterwards I will give you the rifle."

"What if the king should ask for the girl, White Man?"

"Then you shall answer that in the uncertain light you did not recognise her and so she slipped away from you; moreover, that at first you feared to seize the girl lest her cries should alarm the men and they should escape you."

"Good, but how can I be sure that you will give me the gun once you are across the river?"

"Thus: before I enter the ford I will lay the rifle and cartridges upon a stone by the bank, telling Nanea that I shall return to fetch them when I have driven over the cattle."

"It is well, White Man; I will not fail you."

So the plot was made, and after some further conversation upon points of detail, the two conspirators shook hands and parted.

"That ought to come off all right," reflected Hadden to himself as he plunged and floated in the waters of the stream, "but somehow I don't quite trust our friend Maputa. It would have been better if I could have relied upon myself to get rid of Nahoon and his respected uncle— a couple of shots would do it in the water. But then that would be murder and murder is unpleasant; whereas the other thing is only the delivery to justice of two base deserters, a laudable action in a military country. Also personal interference upon my part might turn the girl against me; while after Umgona and Nahoon have been wiped out by Maputa, she *must* accept my escort. Of course there is a risk, but in every walk of life the most cautious have to take risks at times."

As it chanced, Philip Hadden was correct in his suspicions of his coadjutor, Maputa. Even before that worthy chief reached his own kraal, he had come to the conclusion that the white man's plan, though attractive in some ways, was too dangerous, since it was certain that if the girl Nanea escaped, the king would be indignant. Moreover, the men he took with him to do the killing in the drift would suspect something and talk. On the other hand he would earn much credit with his majesty by revealing the plot, saying that he had learned it from the lips of the white hunter, whom Umgona and Nahoon had forced to participate in it, and of whose coveted rifle he must trust to chance to possess himself.

*　　*　　*

An hour later two discreet messengers were bounding across the plains, bearing words from the Chief Maputa, the Warden of the Border, to the "great Black Elephant" at Ulundi.

CHAPTER V

THE DOOM POOL

Fortune showed itself strangely favourable to the plans of Nahoon and Nanea. One of the Zulu captain's perplexities was as to how he should lull the suspicions and evade the vigilance of his own companions, who together with himself had been detailed by the king to assist Hadden in his hunting and to guard against his escape. As it chanced, however, on the day after the incident of the visit of Maputa, a messenger arrived from no less a person than the great military Induna, Tvingwayo ka Marolo, who afterwards commanded the Zulu army at Isandhlwana, ordering these men to return to their regiment, the Umcityu Corps, which was to be placed upon full war footing. Accordingly Nahoon sent them, saying that he himself would follow with Black Heart in the course of a few days, as at present the white man was not sufficiently recovered from his hurts to allow of his travelling fast and far. So the soldiers went, doubting nothing.

Then Umgona gave it out that in obedience to the command of the king he was about to start for Ulundi, taking with him his daughter Nanea to be delivered over into the *Sigodhla*, and also those fifteen head of cattle that had been *lobola'd* by Nahoon in consideration of his forthcoming marriage, whereof he had been fined by Cetywayo. Under pretence that they required a change of veldt, the rest of his cattle he sent away in charge of a Basuto herd who knew nothing of their plans, telling him to keep them by the Crocodile Drift, as there the grass was good and sweet.

All preparations being completed, on the third day the party started, heading straight for Ulundi. After they had travelled some miles, however, they left the road and turning sharp to the right, passed unobserved of any through a great stretch of uninhabited bush. Their path now lay not far from the Pool of Doom, which, indeed, was close to Umgona's kraal, and the forest that was called Home of the Dead, but out of sight of these. It was their plan to travel by night, reaching the broken country near the Crocodile Drift on the following morning. Here they proposed to lie hid that day and through the night; then, having first collected the cattle which had preceded them, to cross the river at the break of dawn and escape into Natal. At least this was the plan of his companions; but, as we know, Hadden had another programme, whereon after one last appearance two of the party would play no part.

During that long afternoon's journey Umgona, who knew every inch of the country, walked ahead driving the fifteen cattle and carrying in his hand a long travelling stick of black and white *umzimbeet* wood, for in truth the old man was in a hurry to reach his journey's end. Next came Nahoon, armed with a broad assegai, but naked except for his moocha and necklet of baboon's teeth, and with him Nanea in her white bead-bordered mantle. Hadden, who brought up the rear, noticed that the girl seemed to be under the spell of an imminent apprehension, for from time to time she clasped her lover's arm, and looking up into his face, addressed him with vehemence, almost with passion.

Curiously enough, the sight touched Hadden, and once or twice he was shaken by so sharp a pang of remorse at the thought of his share in this tragedy, that he cast about in his mind seeking a means to unravel the web of death which he himself had woven. But ever that evil voice was whispering at

his ear. It reminded him that he, the white *Inkoos*, had been refused by this dusky beauty, and that if he found a way to save
him, within some few hours she would be the wife of the savage
gentleman at her side, the man who had named him Black Heart
and who despised him, the man whom he had meant to murder
and who immediately repaid his treachery by rescuing him from
the jaws of the leopard at the risk of his own life. Moreover, it was
a law of Hadden's existence never to deny himself of anything
that he desired if it lay within his power to take it—a law which
had led him always deeper into sin. In other respects, indeed, it
had not carried him far, for in the past he had not desired much,
and he had won little; but this particular flower was to his hand,
and he would pluck it. If Nahoon stood between him and the
flower, so much the worse for Nahoon, and if it should wither in
his grasp, so much the worse for the flower; it could always be
thrown away. Thus it came about that, not for the first time in
his life, Philip Hadden discarded the somewhat spasmodic
prickings of conscience and listened to that evil whispering at his
ear.

About half-past five o'clock in the afternoon the four refu-
gees passed the stream that a mile or so down fell over the little
precipice into the Doom Pool; and, entering a patch of thorn trees
on the further side, walked straight into the midst of two-and-
twenty soldiers, who were beguiling the tedium of expectancy by
the taking of snuff and the smoking of *dakka* or native hemp.
With these soldiers, seated on his pony, for he was too fat to walk,
waited the Chief Maputa.

Observing that their expected guests had arrived, the men
knocked out the *dakka* pipe, replaced the snuff boxes in the slits
made in the lobes of their ears, and secured the four of them.

"What is the meaning of this, O King's soldiers?" asked
Umgona in a quavering voice. "We journey to the kraal of
U'Cetywayo; why do you molest us?"

"Indeed. Wherefore then are your faces set towards the
south. Does the Black One live in the south? Well, you will journey to another kraal presently," answered the jovial-looking cap-

tain of the party with a callous laugh.

"I do not understand," stammered Umgona.

"Then I will explain while you rest," said the captain. "The Chief Maputa yonder sent word to the Black One at Ulundi that he had learned of your intended flight to Natal from the lips of this white man, who had warned him of it. The Black One was angry, and despatched us to catch you and make an end of you. That is all. Come on now, quietly, and let us finish the matter. As the Doom Pool is near, your deaths will be easy."

Nahoon heard the words, and sprang straight at the throat of Hadden; but he did not reach it, for the soldiers pulled him down. Nanea heard them also, and turning, looked the traitor in the eyes; she said nothing, she only looked, but he could never forget that look. The white man for his part was filled with a fiery indignation against Maputa.

"You wicked villain," he gasped, whereat the chief smiled in a sickly fashion, and turned away.

Then they were marched along the banks of the stream till they reached the waterfall that fell into the Pool of Doom.

Hadden was a brave man after his fashion, but his heart quailed as he gazed into that abyss.

"Are you going to throw me in there?" he asked of the Zulu captain in a thick voice.

"You, White Man?" replied the soldier unconcernedly. "No, our orders are to take you to the king, but what he will do with you I do not know. There is to be war between your people and ours, so perhaps he means to pound you into medicine for the use of the witch-doctors, or to peg you over an ant-heap as a warning to other white men."

Hadden received this information in silence, but its effect upon his brain was bracing, for instantly he began to search out some means of escape.

By now the party had halted near the two thorn trees that hung over the waters of the pool.

"Who dives first," asked the captain of the Chief Maputa.

"The old wizard," he replied, nodding at Umgona; "then his

daughter after him, and last of all this fellow," and he struck Nahoon in the face with his open hand.

"Come on, Wizard," said the captain, grasping Umgona by the arm, "and let us see how you can swim."

At the words of doom Umgona seemed to recover his self-command, after the fashion of his race.

"No need to lead me, soldier," he said, shaking himself loose, "who am old and ready to die." Then he kissed his daughter at his side, wrung Nahoon by the hand, and turning from Hadden with a gesture of contempt walked out upon the platform that joined the two thorn trunks. Here he stood for a moment looking at the setting sun, then suddenly, and without a sound, he hurled himself into the abyss below and vanished.

"That was a brave one," said the captain with admiration. "Can you spring too, girl, or must we throw you?"

"I can walk my father's path," Nanea answered faintly, "but first I crave leave to say one word. It is true that we were escaping from the king, and therefore by the law we must die; but it was Black Heart here who made the plot, and he who has betrayed us. Would you know why he has betrayed us? Because he sought my favour, and I refused him, and this is the vengeance that he takes—a white man's vengeance."

"Wow!" broke in the chief Maputa, "this pretty one speaks truth, for the white man would have made a bargain with me under which Umgona, the wizard, and Nahoon, the soldier, were to be killed at the Crocodile Drift, and he himself suffered to escape with the girl. I spoke him softly and said 'yes,' and then like a loyal man I reported to the king."

"You hear," sighed Nanea. "Nahoon, fare you well, though presently perhaps we shall be together again. It was I who tempted you from your duty. For my sake you forgot your honour, and I am repaid. Farewell, my husband, it is better to die with you than to enter the house of the king's women," and Nanea stepped on to the platform.

Here, holding to a bough of one of the thorn trees, she turned and addressed Hadden, saying:

"Black Heart, you seem to have won the day, but me at least you lose and—the sun is not yet set. After sunset comes the night, Black Heart, and in that night I pray that you may wander eternally, and be given to drink of my blood and the blood of Umgona my father, and the blood of Nahoon my husband, who saved your life, and whom you have murdered. Perchance, Black Heart, we may yet meet yonder—in the House of the Dead."

Then uttering a low cry Nanea clasped her hands and sprang upwards and outwards from the platform. The watchers bent their heads forward to look. They saw her rush headlong down the face of the fall to strike the water fifty feet below. A few seconds, and for the last time, they caught sight of her white garment glimmering on the surface of the gloomy pool. Then the shadows and mist-wreaths hid it, and she was gone.

"Now, husband," cried the cheerful voice of the captain, "yonder is your marriage bed, so be swift to follow a bride who is so ready to lead the way. *Wow!* But you are good people to kill; never have I had to do with any who gave less trouble. You—" and he stopped, for mental agony had done its work, and suddenly Nahoon went mad before his eyes.

With a roar like that of a lion the great man cast off those who held him and seizing one of them round the waist and thigh, he put out all his terrible strength. Lifting him as though he had been an infant, he hurled him over the edge of the cliff to find his death on the rocks of the Pool of Doom. Then crying:

"Black Heart! Your turn, Black Heart the traitor!" he rushed at Hadden, his eyes rolling and foam flying from his lips, as he passed striking the chief Maputa from his horse with a backward blow of his hand. Ill would it have gone with the white man if Nahoon had caught him. But he could not come at him, for the soldiers sprang upon him and notwithstanding his fearful struggles they pulled him to the ground, as at certain festivals the Zulu regiments with their naked hands pull down a bull in the presence of the king.

"Cast him over before he can work more mischief," said a

voice. But the captain cried out, "Nay, nay, he is sacred; the fire from Heaven has fallen on his brain, and we may not harm him, else evil would overtake us all. Bind him hand and foot, and bear him tenderly to where he can be cared for. Surely I thought that these evil-doers were giving us too little trouble, and thus it has proved."

So they set themselves to make fast Nahoon's hands and wrists, using as much gentleness as they might, for among the Zulus a lunatic is accounted holy. It was no easy task, and it took time.

Hadden glanced around him, and saw his opportunity. On the ground close beside him lay his rifle, where one of the soldiers had placed it, and about a dozen yards away Maputa's pony was grazing. With a swift movement, he seized the Martini and five seconds later he was on the back of the pony, heading for the Crocodile Drift at a gallop. So quickly indeed did he execute this masterly retreat, that occupied as they all were in binding Nahoon, for half a minute or more none of the soldiers noticed what had happened. Then Maputa chanced to see, and waddled after him to the top of the rise, screaming:

"The white thief, he has stolen my horse, and the gun too, the gun that he promised to give me."

Hadden, who by this time was a hundred yards away, heard him clearly, and a rage filled his heart. This man had made an open murderer of him; more, he had been the means of robbing him of the girl for whose sake he had dipped his hands in these iniquities. He glanced over his shoulder; Maputa was still running, and alone. Yes, there was time; at any rate he would risk it.

Pulling up the pony with a jerk, he leapt from its back, slipping his arm through the rein with an almost simultaneous movement. As it chanced, and as he had hoped would be the case, the animal was a trained shooting horse, and stood still. Hadden planted his feet firmly on the ground and drawing a deep breath, he cocked the rifle and covered the advancing chief. Now Maputa saw his purpose and with a yell of terror turned to fly. Hadden waited a second to get the sight fair on his broad back, then just as the soldiers appeared above the rise he pressed the trigger. He was a noted shot, and in this instance his skill did not fail him; for, before he heard the bullet tell, Maputa flung his arms wide and plunged to the ground dead.

Three seconds more, and with a savage curse, Hadden had remounted the pony and was riding for his life towards the river, which a while later he crossed in safety.

CHAPTER VI

THE GHOST OF THE DEAD

When Nanea leapt from the dizzy platform that overhung the Pool of Doom, a strange fortune befell her. Close in to the precipice were many jagged rocks, and on these the waters of the fall fell and thundered, bounding from them in spouts of spray into the troubled depths of the foss beyond. It was on these stones that the life was dashed out from the bodies of the wretched victims who were hurled from above. But Nanea, it will be remembered, had not waited to be treated thus, and as it chanced the strong spring with which she had leapt to death carried her clear of the rocks. By a very little she missed the edge of them and striking the deep water head first like some practised diver, she sank down and down till she thought that she would never rise again. Yet she did rise, at the end of the pool in the mouth of the rapid, along which she sped swiftly, carried down by the rush of the water. Fortunately there were no rocks here; and, since she was a skilful swimmer, she escaped the danger of being thrown against the banks.

For a long distance she was borne thus till at length she saw that she was in a forest, for trees cut off the light from the water, and their drooping branches swept its surface. One of these Nanea caught with her hand, and by the help of it she dragged herself from the River of Death whence none had escaped before. Now she stood upon the bank gasping but quite unharmed; there was not a scratch on her body; even her white garment was still fast about her neck.

But though she had suffered no hurt in her terrible voyage, so exhausted was Nanea that she could scarcely stand. Here the gloom was that of night, and shivering with cold she looked helplessly to find some refuge. Close to the water's edge grew an enormous yellow-wood tree, and to this she staggered—thinking to climb it, and seek shelter in its boughs where, as she hoped, she would be safe from wild beasts. Again fortune befriended her, for at a distance of a few feet from the ground there was a great hole in the tree which, she discovered, was hollow. Into this hole she crept, taking her chance of its being the home of snakes or other evil creatures, to find that the interior was wide and warm. It was dry also, for at the bottom of the cavity lay a foot or more of rotten tinder and moss brought there by rats or birds. Upon this tinder she lay down, and covering herself with the moss and leaves soon sank into sleep or stupor.

How long Nanea slept she did not know, but at length she was awakened by a sound as of guttural human voices talking in a language that she could not understand. Rising to her knees she peered out of the hole in the tree. It was night, but the stars shone brilliantly, and their light fell upon an open circle of ground close by the edge of the river. In this circle there burned a great fire, and at a little distance from the fire were gathered eight or ten horrible-looking beings, who appeared to be rejoicing over something that lay upon the ground. They were small in stature, men and women together, but no children, and all of them were nearly naked. Their hair was long and thin, growing down almost to the eyes, their jaws and teeth protruded and the girth of their black bodies was out of all proportion to their height. In their hands they held sticks with sharp stones lashed on to them, or rude hatchet-like knives of the same material.

Now Nanea's heart shrank within her, and she nearly fainted with fear, for she knew that she was in the haunted forest, and without a doubt these were the *Esemkofu*, the evil ghosts that dwelt therein. Yes, that was what they were, and yet she could not take her eyes off them —the sight of them held her with a horrible fascination. But if they were ghosts, why did they sing and dance like men? Why did they wave those sharp stones aloft, and quarrel and strike each other? And why did they make a fire as men do when they wish to cook food? More, what was it that they rejoiced over, that long dark thing which lay so quiet upon the ground? It did not look like a head of game, and it could scarcely be a crocodile, yet clearly it was food of some sort, for they were sharpening the stone knives in order to cut it up.

While she wondered thus, one of the dreadful-looking little creatures advanced to the fire, and taking from it a burning bough, held it over the thing that lay upon the ground, to give light to a companion who was about to do something to it with the stone knife. Next instant Nanea drew back her head from the hole, a stifled shriek upon her lips. She saw what it was now—it was the body of a man. Yes, and these were no ghosts; they were cannibals of whom when she was little, her mother had told her tales to keep her from wandering away from home.

But who was the man they were about to eat? It could not be one of themselves, for his stature was much greater. Oh! Now she knew; it must be Nahoon, who had been killed up yonder, and whose dead body the waters had brought down to the haunted forest as they had brought her alive. Yes, it must be Nahoon, and she would be forced to see her husband devoured before her eyes. The thought of it overwhelmed her. That he should die by order of the king was natural, but that he should be buried thus! Yet what could she do to prevent it? Well, if it cost her her life, it should be prevented. At the worst they could only kill and eat her also, and now that Nahoon and her father were gone, being untroubled by any religious or spiritual hopes and fears, she was not greatly concerned to keep her own breath in her.

Slipping through the hole in the tree, Nanea walked quietly towards the cannibals—not knowing in the least what she should do when she reached them. As she arrived in line with the fire this lack of programme came home to her mind forcibly, and she paused to reflect. Just then one of the cannibals looked up to see a tall and stately figure wrapped in a white garment which, as the flame-light flickered on it, seemed now to advance from the dense background of shadow, and now to recede into it. The poor savage wretch was holding a stone knife in his teeth when he beheld her, but it did not remain there long, for opening his great jaws he uttered the most terrified and piercing yell that Nanea had ever heard. Then the others saw her also, and presently the forest was ringing with shrieks of fear. For a few seconds the outcasts stood and gazed, then they were gone this way and that, bursting their path through the undergrowth like startled jackals. The *Esemkofu* of Zulu tradition had been routed in their own haunted home by what they took to be a spirit.

Poor *Esemkofu!* They were but miserable and starving bushmen who, driven into that place of ill omen many years ago, had adopted this means, the only one open to them, to keep the life in their wretched bodies. Here at least they were unmolested, and as there was little other food to be found amid that wilderness of trees, they took what the river brought them. When executions were few in the Pool of Doom, times were hard for them indeed—for then they were driven to eat each other. That is why there were no children.

As their inarticulate outcry died away in the distance, Nanea ran forward to look at the body that lay on the ground, and staggered back with a sigh of relief. It was not Nahoon, but she recognised the face for that of one of the party of executioners. How did he come here? Had Nahoon killed him? Had Nahoon escaped? She could not tell, and at the best it was improbable, but still the sight of this dead soldier lit her heart with a faint ray of hope, for how did he come to be dead if Nahoon had no hand in his death? She could not bear to leave him lying so near her hiding-place, however; therefore, with no small toil, she rolled the corpse back into the water, which carried it swiftly away. Then she returned to the tree, having first replenished the fire, and awaited the light.

At last it came—so much of it as ever penetrated this

darksome den— and Nanea, becoming aware that she was hungry, descended from the tree to search for food. All day long she searched, finding nothing, till towards sunset she remembered that on the outskirts of the forest there was a flat rock where it was the custom of those who had been in any way afflicted, or who considered themselves or their belongings to be bewitched, to place propitiatory offerings of food wherewith the *Esemkofu* and *Amalhosi* were supposed to satisfy their spiritual cravings. Urged by the pinch of starvation, to this spot Nanea journeyed rapidly, and found to her joy that some neighbouring kraal had evidently been in recent trouble, for the Rock of Offering was laden with cobs of corn, gourds of milk, porridge and even meat. Helping herself to as much as she could carry, she returned to her lair, where she drank of the milk and cooked meat and mealies at the fire. Then she crept back into the tree, and slept.

For nearly two months Nanea lived thus in the forest, since she could not venture out of it—fearing lest she should be seized, and for a second time taste of the judgment of the king. In the forest at least she was safe, for none dared enter there, nor did the *Esemkofu* give her further trouble. Once or twice she saw them, but on each occasion they fled from her presence—seeking some distant retreat, where they hid themselves or perished. Nor did food fail her, for finding that it was taken, the pious givers brought it in plenty to the Rock of Offering.

But, oh! The life was dreadful, and the gloom and loneliness coupled with her sorrows at times drove her almost to insanity. Still she lived on, though often she desired to die, for if her father was dead, the corpse she had found was not the corpse of Nahoon, and in her heart there still shone that spark of home. Yet what she hoped for she could not tell.

*   *   *

When Philip Hadden reached civilised regions, he found that war was about to be declared between the Queen and Cetywayo, King of the Amazulu; also that in the prevailing excitement his little adventure with the Utrecht store-keeper had been overlooked or forgotten. He was the owner of two good buck-waggons with spans of salted oxen, and at that time vehicles were much in request to carry military stores for the columns which were to advance into Zululand; indeed the transport authorities were glad to pay £90 a month for the hire of each waggon and to guarantee the owners against all loss of cattle. Although he was not desirous of returning to Zululand, this bait proved too much for Hadden, who accordingly leased out his waggons to the Commissariat, together with his own services as conductor and interpreter.

He was attached to No. 3 column of the invading force, which it may be remembered was under the immediate command of Lord Chelmsford, and on the 20th of January, 1879, he marched with it by the road that runs from Rorke's Drift to the Indeni forest, and encamped that night beneath the shadow of the steep and desolate mountain known as Isandhlwana.

That day also a great army of King Cetywayo's, numbering twenty thousand men and more, moved down from the Upindo Hill and camped upon the stony plain that lies a mile and a half to the east of Isandhlwana. No fires were lit, and it lay there in utter silence, for the warriors were "sleeping on their spears."

With that *impi* was the Umcityu regiment, three thousand five hundred strong. At the first break of dawn the Induna in command of the Umcityu looked up from beneath the shelter of the black shield with which he had covered his body, and through the thick mist he saw a great man standing before him, clothed only in a moocha, a gaunt wild-eyed man who held a rough club in his hand. When he was spoken to, the man made no answer; he only leaned upon his club looking from left to right along the dense array of innumerable shields.

"Who is this *Silwana* (wild creature)?" asked the Induna of his captains wondering.

The captains stared at the wanderer, and one of them replied, "This is Nahoon-ka-Zomba, it is the son of Zomba who not long ago held rank in this regiment of the Umcityu. His betrothed, Nanea, daughter of Umgona, was killed together with her father by order of the Black One, and Nahoon went mad with grief at the sight of it, for the fire of Heaven entered his brain, and mad he has wandered ever since."

"What would you here, Nahoon-ka-Zomba?" asked the Induna.

Then Nahoon spoke slowly. "My regiment goes down to war against the white men; give me a shield and a spear, O Captain of the king, that I may fight with my regiment, for I seek a face in the battle."

So they gave him a shield and a spear, for they dared not turn away one whose brain was alight with the fire of Heaven.

*   *   *

When the sun was high that day, bullets began to fall among the ranks of the Umcityu. Then the black-shielded, black-plumed Umcityu arose, company by company, and after them arose the whole vast Zulu army, breast and horns together, and swept down in silence upon the doomed British camp, a moving sheen of spears. The bullets pattered on the shields, the shells tore long lines through their array, but they never halted or wavered. Forward on either side shot out the horns of armed men, clasping the camp in an embrace of steel. Then as these began to close, out burst the war cry of the Zulus, and with the roar of a torrent and the rush of a storm, with a sound like the humming of a billion bees, wave after wave the deep breast of the *impi* rolled down upon the white men. With it went the black-shielded Umcityu and with them went Nahoon, the son of Zomba. A bullet struck him in the side, glancing from his ribs, he did not heed; a white man fell from his horse before him, he did not stab, for he sought but one face in the battle.

He sought—and at last he found. There, among the waggons where the spears were busiest, there standing by his horse and firing rapidly was Black Heart, he who had given Nanea his betrothed to death. Three soldiers stood between them, one of them Nahoon stabbed, and two he brushed aside; then he rushed straight at Hadden.

But the white man saw him come, and even through the mask of his madness he knew Nahoon again, and terror took hold of him. Throwing away his empty rifle, for his ammunition was spent, he leaped upon his horse and drove his spurs into its flanks. Away it went among the carnage, springing over the dead and bursting through the lines of shields, and after it came Nahoon, running long and low with head stretched forward and trailing spear, running as a hound runs when the buck is at view.

Hadden's first plan was to head for Rorke's Drift, but a glance to the left showed him that the masses of the Undi barred that way, so he fled straight on, leaving his path to fortune. In five minutes he was over a ridge, and there was nothing of the battle to be seen, in ten all sounds of it had died away, for few guns were fired in the dread race to Fugitive's Drift, and the assegai makes no noise. In some strange fashion, even at this moment, the contrast between the dreadful scene of blood and turmoil that he had left, and the peaceful face of Nature over which he was passing, came home to his brain vividly. Here birds sang and cattle grazed; here the sun shone undimmed by the smoke of cannon, only high up in the blue and silent air long streams of vultures could be seen winging their way to the Plain of Isandhlwana.

The ground was very rough, and Hadden's horse began to tire. He looked over his shoulder—there some two hundred yards behind came the Zulu, grim as Death, unswerving as Fate. He examined the pistol in his belt; there was but one undischarged cartridge left, all the rest had been fired and the pouch was empty. Well, one bullet should be enough for one savage: the question was should he stop and use it now? No, he might miss or fail to kill the man; he was on horseback and his foe on foot, surely he could tire him out.

A while passed, and they dashed through a little stream. It seemed familiar to Hadden. Yes, that was the pool where he used to bathe when he was the guest of Umgona, the father of Nanea; and there on the knoll to his right were the huts, or rather the remains of them, for they had been burnt with fire. What chance had brought him to this place, he wondered; then again he looked behind him at Nahoon, who seemed to read his thoughts, for he shook his spear and pointed to the ruined kraal.

On he went at speed for here the land was level, and to his joy he lost sight of his pursuer. But presently there came a mile of rocky ground, and when it was past, glancing back he saw that Nahoon was once more in his old place. His horse's strength was almost spent, but Hadden spurred it forward blindly, whither he knew not. Now he was travelling along a strip of turf and ahead of him he heard the music of a river, while to his left rose a high bank. Presently the turf bent inwards and there, not twenty yards away from him, was a Kaffir hut standing on the brink of a river. He looked at it, yes, it was the hut of that accursed *inyanga*, the Bee, and standing by the fence of it was none other than the Bee herself. At the sight of her the exhausted horse swerved violently, stumbled and came to the ground, where it lay panting. Hadden was thrown from the saddle but sprang to his feet unhurt.

"Ah! Black Heart, is it you? What news of the battle, Black Heart?" cried the Bee in a mocking voice.

"Help me, mother, I am pursued," he gasped.

"What of it, Black Heart, it is but by one tired man. Stand then and face him, for now Black Heart and White Heart are together again. You will not? Then away to the forest and seek shelter among the dead who await you there. Tell me, tell me, was it the face of Nanea that I saw beneath the waters a while ago? Good! Bear my greetings to her when you two meet in the House of the Dead."

Hadden looked at the stream; it was in flood. He could not swim it, so followed by the evil laugh of the prophetess, he sped towards the forest. After him came Nahoon, his tongue hanging from his jaws like the tongue of a wolf.

Now he was in the shadow of the forest, but still he sped on following the course of the river, till at length his breath failed, and he halted on the further side of a little glade, beyond which a great tree grew. Nahoon was more than a spear's throw behind him; therefore he had time to draw his pistol and make ready.

"Halt, Nahoon," he cried, as once before he had cried; "I would speak with you."

The Zulu heard his voice, and obeyed.

"Listen," said Hadden. "We have run a long race and fought a long fight, you and I, and we are still alive both of us. Very soon, if you come on, one of us must be dead, and it will be you, Nahoon, for I am armed and as you know I can shoot straight. What do you say?"

Nahoon made no answer, but stood still at the edge of the glade, his wild and glowering eyes fixed on the white man's face and his breath coming in short gasps.

"Will you let me go, if *I* let *you* go?" Hadden asked once more. "I know why you hate me, but the past cannot be undone, nor can the dead be brought to earth again."

Still Nahoon made no answer, and his silence seemed more fateful and more crushing than any speech; no spoken accusation would have been so terrible in Hadden's ear. He made no answer, but lifting his assegai he stalked grimly toward his foe.

When he was within five paces Hadden covered him and fired. Nahoon sprang aside, but the bullet struck him somewhere, for his right arm dropped, and the stabbing spear that he held was jerked from it harmlessly over the white man's head. But still making no sound, the Zulu came on and gripped him by the throat with his left hand. For a space they struggled terribly, swaying to and fro, but Hadden was unhurt and fought with the fury of despair, while Nahoon had been twice wounded, and there remained to him but one sound arm wherewith to strike. Presently forced to earth by the white man's iron strength, the soldier was down, nor could he rise again.

"Now we will make an end," muttered Hadden savagely, and he turned to seek the assegai, then staggered slowly back with starting eyes and reeling gait. For there before him, still clad in her white robe, a spear in her hand, stood the spirit of Nanea!

"Think of it," he said to himself, dimly remembering the words of the *inyanga*, "when you stand face to face with the ghost of the dead in the Home of the Dead."

There was a cry and a flash of steel; the broad spear leapt towards him to bury itself in his breast. He swayed, he fell, and presently Black Heart clasped that great reward which the word of the Bee had promised Him.

*　　*　　*

"Nahoon! Nahoon!" murmured a soft voice, "awake, it is no ghost, but I —Nanea—I, your living wife, to whom my Ehlose[7] has given it me to save you."

Nahoon heard and opened his eyes to look and his madness left him.

"Welcome, wife," he said faintly, "now I will live since Death has brought you back to me in the House of the Dead."

*　　*　　*

To-day Nahoon is one of the Indunas of the English Government in Zululand, and there are children about his kraal. It was from the lips of none other than Nanea his wife that the teller of this tale heard its substance.

The Bee also lives and practises as much magic as she dares under the white man's rule. On her black hand shines a golden ring shaped like a snake with ruby eyes, and of this trinket the Bee is very proud.

7 Guardian Spirit.

Lightning Source UK Ltd.
Milton Keynes UK
11 March 2011

169097UK00002B/68/A